To

Cian

Within Their
Screams

Chris Rush

Don't become his
Victim!

Acknowledgements

I want to say a huge thanks to you for taking the time to read my work. Your support really means a lot and I hope you enjoy this book.

My thanks to Lisa V. Proulx, Indie Author Consulting, for editing this book and being there for all my questions.

Thanks to All Things Rotten for creating an amazing cover.

A special thanks to Tina Barcoe for continuing to support and promote me every chance she gets.

Finally, thank you to all my friends and family out there, you all know who you are, your time and support means everything!

"If you scream needlessly for help, I will smash your teeth and pull what's left of them from your mouth with this," Darren Kelly.

Chapter 1

The cold rain patted gently against the window, as Darren sat in his bedroom staring blankly at the wall in front of him.

He had spent the previous half hour trying to dilute the memories of his childhood as they continued to advance through his mind, as they did so on many occasions.

Words like *freak, weirdo* and *monster* haunted him for many years growing up and even now, having just turned twenty, he would still be the subject of many conversations within the community.

Darren had a rather sheltered childhood due to being born with a rare condition which made him immune to feeling physical pain of any kind. Once diagnosed, it meant his parents had to be extra vigilant when he was a child. Injuries could go unnoticed and in turn become infected or never heal if not treated correctly or in time.

His parents William and Sarah, whom he still lived with, tried their utmost to allow him live as normal a life as possible. They witnessed many times, Darren smiling and continuing to play, when another child would be on the ground crying due to the injury they sustained. However, once word of his condition spread through the local school, the bullying by the other children became too much, and eventually the decision was made to continue his education from home. Sarah and William always praised the teachers for doing their best to keep Darren's condition as private as possible and for how they looked after him while he was in their care, however they couldn't dedicate their entire day to him as they had other students to teach.

Older now, Darren had a better understanding of how to live with and manage his condition. He had to be vigilant after any physical knocks or bangs to his body, or after being exposed to anything which may normally cause a person harm.

Although his parents often told him to treat a painless life as a gift, he viewed it as a curse. Over the years he longed to experience and understand more of what pain was, what it did to the human body and why people reacted the way they did to this alien feeling.

"Dinner love!" called a voice from downstairs, snapping Darren from his daydream.

He stood, cast his common thoughts aside, and made his way through the house which was decorated with many photographs of him when he was younger and old ornaments which his parents loved to collect. Darren often looked at pictures of himself smiling as a child, the younger version of himself totally unaware of just how different he was.

Stepping into the kitchen, Darren was greeted with a huge smile and loving eyes.

"I thought you were asleep up there," Sarah said, placing his dinner before him on the table.

"No, just thinking," Darren replied, taking a seat.

"Everything okay?" His mother asked, wiping her thin, bony hands in the towel dangling from her apron, before she began to prepare his father's meal, who was due home from his part-time job soon.

"Fine thanks, you know me, I'm always good," Darren smiled, placing a fork full of meat into his mouth.

Sarah couldn't help but notice the sarcasm in his tone and said, "I'm always here if you ever want to talk."

"Of course. Don't worry. I'm okay," Darren replied not raising his head from the table.

Although he always had everything his parents could possibly provide for him, Darren felt something was always missing. Unable to experience pain made him feel he was in some way disconnected from witnessing what it was like to be human. He knew he was viewed as someone different in the community and over the years had come to consider himself dissimilar to the people around him.

Moments later the back door opened, and William stepped into the kitchen, giving his wife a kiss on the cheek.

"How are you today?" The tall, slender man asked, turning and sitting across from Darren.

"I'm good, how was work?" Darren replied, deflecting the question back to his father.

William paused a moment and looked down towards his son's right hand. Darren discreetly had the tip of the sharp steak knife placed against his thumb and was pushing so hard William was sure it was about to burst through the other side at any moment, splitting the thumbnail and slicing the tip of the digit in two in the process. Darren quickly eyed his father's stare and instantly stopped the activity. Over the years Sarah and William had witnessed their son place himself in dangerous situations and carry out hazardous acts, which if went unhindered, would have resulted in disastrous consequences for him and total distress for his parents.

"Oh great, I can't wait to go back tomorrow," he laughed across the table, to try steer his son's mood towards a happier one.

"I bet you can't," Darren smiled back towards William.

Darren loved his aging parents, he cared for them as much as they did him, however there was a growing urge building inside him, he wanted to experience something which he knew he could never achieve.

"Smartarse, it's hard work you know," William replied with a huge grin cracked across his wrinkled face. Nearing retiring age, William worked three hours a day in a local hardware shop which was within walking distance from the house.

"Stop now boys or I'll have to get involved," Sarah laughed, finally sitting down beside them to enjoy her dinner.

"That's telling us isn't it," Darren giggled, as he and his father burst into a loud laughter.

After the family enjoyed their meal, Darren helped his mother with the washing up and went back upstairs to his bedroom.

"Does he seem okay to you?" William asked Sarah as she joined him on the large sofa in the sitting room. "He has been a little quite lately."

"Yeah I've noticed that too. We should keep an eye on him over the next couple of days eh?" William suggested.

"Yeah that's a good idea. I'll see how he is in the morning, it can't be easy having basically no one to turn to at his age," Sarah said, worry beginning to build within her as it had so many times over the years.

Meanwhile Darren stood motionless in his bedroom listening to the rain, stab, hard now, against the glass beside him. He turned and looked at his reflection in the large mirror to his right. He raised his left hand, took hold of a piece of skin on his neck and began to pull. Witnessing the flesh stretch farther and farther, Darren could feel nothing. No sensation, no indication that anything was hurting him, no feeling whatsoever. However, he knew if anyone else tried the same activity, they would eventually have to submit to the pain involved.

Sighing loudly, Darren released the skin, switched off the bedroom light and climbed into bed.

Staring at the ceiling, he wanted nothing more than to feel as everyone else did. To him pain was the forbidden fruit which he would never be able to taste. He remembered when he was younger, falling so many times and never once needed to run to his parents for comfort. Although the cuts and bruises would be present on him, there was no internal warning feature to prevent him from doing the same thing which caused the injury all over again. This of course was something the other children he grew up around with found very strange and, at times frightening. William and Sarah wanted their son to have a normal life as much as possible, however with each fall came an in-depth medical assessment and monitoring to ensure that Darren had not, first of all, seriously injured himself and any unknown wounds were not becoming infected.

Hearing his parents go to bed later that night, Darren knew without any doubt his parents loved him, yet he couldn't help allowing the thought of their age leading him to believe he was a gnawing burden on them.

He, in the past, contributed towards the household to help his parents, but following a number of accidents at work, one of which left a huge laceration on his upper arm unnoticed until he saw his blood all over the warehouse equipment, Darren's former employer and parents thought it better he if quit, rather than another, more serious, life threatening injury go overlooked. It was a tough decision for

Darren because he enjoyed his job. He had started taking driving lessons, afterwards obtaining a full driver's license, with the intention of progressing further within the company, so the job loss had a huge impact on his confidence.

Seeing his torn flesh and blood running from him due to the countless wounds over the years always felt surreal to Darren without any painful consequence. He had seen others fall, suffer cuts, bruises, bleed and he could never understand what it felt like to trigger their reaction due to feeling the one thing he couldn't.

Before he knew it, it was once again the early hours of the morning. Over several weeks, Darren found himself wandering away in his thoughts while time raced by around him. He shuffled slightly on the soft mattress beneath him, repositioned his temple against the double set of pillows and closed his eyes.

Chapter 2

"How was he this morning?" William asked, double checking Darren hadn't overheard him while he sat and watched television in the sitting room.

"He seemed fine. I didn't ask too many questions, but I did make sure he knows we are here if he ever needs to talk," Sarah said, handing her husband a cup of tea.

"That's good, I thought—"

Without warning there was a loud smash behind William, which caused Darren to race into the kitchen.

Turning, William saw Sarah had dropped a glass and was beginning to pick it up.

"Careful now love, I'll get the brush," William said, referring to the sharp pieces she was collecting in her old hands.

Seconds later Sarah winced as a small shard entered her withering palm causing the blood to instantly pour to the tiled floor beneath her.

As she removed the sharp piece of glass from her flesh, Sarah saw Darren quickly fetch the towel from the handle on the cupboard beneath the sink and come towards her. Whilst he pressed the towel against the wound to help stop the bleeding, Darren studied his mother's grimace and wondered what current feelings she was undergoing to cause the expression and gasps.

When he injured himself and the blood began to pour, he felt no change at all. Darren could literally go about his daily business without knowing anything was wrong except for the visual warning that his internal fluids were leaking from him.

"Are you okay?" William asked, stepping back into the kitchen with a brush to clean up the glass.

"Yeah, I should have just waited for you," Sarah replied, feeling a little silly for cutting herself on something so small.

"Is it sore?" Darren asked, ignoring his father as he began to clean up around their feet.

Sarah concentrated on moving her feet out of William's way rather than replying to her son.

"How does it feel?" Darren continued, while dabbing the towel against the cut, the blood beginning to slow.

"I'm fine, it will take more than that," Sarah said, smiling to Darren.

Darren didn't respond, he maintained his study on his mother's reaction to the sensations she was experiencing. He observed each eyebrow scrunch and eye squint, listened to every sharp inhale of breath and examined each lip movement, knowing that it was something he had never undergone.

"How is it?" William asked, in relation to the cut on his wife's hand.

"It's okay, the bleeding is stopping," Sarah smiled

in response.

Moving the towel away from the broken skin for the final time, Darren looked towards the tiny wound which had caused so many physical responses.

Noticing his parents taking note of his prolonged stare, Darren smiled and placed the towel into the washing machine, then returned to the sitting room to finish watching his television program.

William helped his wife cover the cut with a plaster and then told her to sit down while he switched on the kettle.

Later that evening Sarah and William said good night to Darren and left him watching a movie. Many nights during the week he would stay up late watching television if something interesting caught his attention. He would always be considerate and turn the volume down so his parents could sleep peacefully upstairs, and also as not to disturb their neighbours.

Throughout the evening the thoughts of his mother's injury plagued Darren's mind.

How does something so small, cause someone to react like that? he wondered to himself as he stood and flicked off the switch beside the large television. He always enjoyed watching it in darkness, with the light from the kitchen being the only other source of illumination being cast through the room.

Stepping into the kitchen, Darren turned his attention to the cutlery on the draining board beside the sink and spotted one of the knives used earlier during dinner. Seeing the sharp edge glinting in the light, he couldn't help but make his way over to it. He longed so much over the years to experience the sudden influx of pain even though it was impossible for him. The event earlier had heightened his taste for it a little more, studying his mother's response to the cut on her hand, he desired to know how it felt.

Darren rolled up the sleeve covering his right arm and fetched the knife beside him. Holding his wrist over the sink he placed the tip of the blade against the skin coated in the many scars from years of unnoticed injuries. He placed some pressure on the handle causing an indentation on his forearm. As always there was no sensation whatsoever, had he not been purposefully using the knife, he wouldn't have known any different.

He removed the blade from his flesh and took note of the imprint on his arm. Darren turned the knife and placed the cutting edge against his flesh, applied force and pulled the handle towards him. Immediately the skin sliced open, releasing bright red fluid into the sink.

He sat the knife back onto the draining board and watched the crimson liquid continue to flow from him. He sighed deeply knowing that his body didn't respond to an injury the same as everyone else's. Darren had often contemplated what other emotions he was immune to, however the specialists who had examined him over the years had all reassured him and his family that his condition only effected his pain sensing ability and other physical effects. Emotional pain was still possible.

Listening to the blood pat steadily against the bottom of the sink, Darren positioned his left index and thumb on either side of the cut and pulled it open further, wondering what was missing from him.

Resting his two palms on the sink edge as the blood filled the drain, he paused, thinking himself foolish for obsessing and chasing something unobtainable. After gathering his wandering thoughts, he turned on the tap to allow the water to wash the evidence away. Darren knew his parents would be extremely shocked and concerned if they were to find he carried out such an act.

He held his right forearm under the water and washed away the excess blood. Darren then swiped some sheets of kitchen paper off the roll and pressed them against the wound until the bleeding stopped. He then placed some plasters over it and rolled the sleeve back to its original position. He finished by washing the knife and placed it back onto the draining board. Once he was happy everything was back as it should be, Darren switched off the light and went upstairs to bed.

The following morning Darren awoke and went about his daily, mundane routine, helping around the house. He was sure to conceal the wound he had self-inflicted on himself the night previous as he didn't want to raise any alarm among his parents.

As Darren stepped down the stairs, he heard William say goodbye to Sarah as he left for work. Darren made his way into the kitchen and switched on the kettle.

"Morning dear, raining again today," Sarah said, as she slotted two slices of bread into the toaster.

"Never changes does it?" Darren responded, joining her at the window.

"I have to go to the shop in a bit, you need me to pick you up anything?" Sarah asked, gathering the butter and jam from the fridge, returning to it once more to retrieve an egg carton.

"I can go if you like?" Darren replied.

"No, it's okay, you can stay here," Sarah said, removing the toast from the toaster and laying it on a plate on the table for him.

"Don't worry I can look after myself, you don't need to be with me twenty – four – seven," Darren answered in an irritated tone.

It was true, his parents couldn't watch over him every waking moment, even if they did try their best to attempt it. Darren was a young man and they were getting to an age where they were struggling to get up and down the stairs without falling, something which William was going to address the following summer. He was going to have a downstairs room converted to a bedroom for him and his wife. William and Sarah's biggest fear was when he was out and about, Darren would seriously injure himself in some way and wouldn't get the treatment he needed in time to save his life. The couple had often talked about how rare it would be, but it was certainly possible none the less. This was the main reason he was still being sheltered daily, however Darren was growing ever more frustrated with their over parenting. He loved them dearly, but he wanted to experience things for himself without being nurtured forever.

Knowing they couldn't lock him away in the house, Sarah turned to him and said, "Okay, but I'll come with you so you don't have to try and remember everything," smiling towards him, hoping he wouldn't realise she was using it as an excuse to tag along.

"Okay, we'll go now," Darren said standing from the table.

"No, get your breakfast into you first then we'll go okay," Sarah instructed, as she sat a boiled egg into an eggcup in front of him.

Darren reluctantly sat back down to please his mother.

After breakfast Sarah accompanied Darren to the local shop, just a short walk from their home. They carried out their shopping while receiving a lot of greetings and best wishes from their neighbours seeing him out of the house.

"I'm going to go for a walk," Darren said, on their way back home, the rain deciding to ease somewhat.

Sarah's first impulse was to immediately argue, but what good would it do? She thought, he was an adult and could do what he wanted.

"Have you got your phone with you?" Sarah asked.

"Yes, I have it here," Darren replied, showing it to her, slightly agitated with the question, even though it was something he never used.

"Okay, well, don't go far," Sarah instructed.

Darren rolled his eyes with a smile on his face.

He helped her in with the groceries, gave her a hug and made his way from the house.

Darren turned right and began to walk to the other side of town. Hearing the world move around him gave him a form of release, a sense of normality in a way. He was the same as everyone else, he just didn't feel how others physically felt.

Before he knew it, he was passing alongside the local cemetery. The old, stone walls reached higher towards the sky than he did, and he noticed the two large black steel gates were open. He stepped into the large corpse holding area and listened to the rain runoff make its way through the many surface water drains around him. He was greeted by crosses, holy statues and ornaments decorated on or over the countless graves on display before him. Darren remembered attending funerals of relatives in the past, however a lot more cadavers had been laid to rest in the cemetery since.

He made his way through the showroom of graves, greeted every so often by others who were paying their respects to their lost loved ones. Darren eyed a familiar headstone in the distance, the resting place of his grandfather and grandmother.

He stood at the edge of the grave peering at the writing before him. His grandfather died from a heart attack, his grandmother from cancer.

Darren turned his attention to his surroundings; the first thought was the amount of suffering the site contained within its walls. How many car crashes, falls, illnesses, fires and so forth had resulted in people being laid to rest here and how did it feel to know the they pain endured was leading to the unavoidable end? He wondered, as he walked to his left and took note of the ages displayed on the headstones. Several variances, but they all had one thing in common, they all felt the one thing he couldn't.

"Hello," said an elderly woman removing some weeds from a curb to his right.

Darren smiled and continued towards the gate. He enjoyed the slight freedom getting out of the house but his obsession to experience the unattainable physical hurt everyone else could was growing within him.

The rain slowly began to return to its earlier glory, and Darren didn't want his mother to worry unnecessarily, so he decided to make his way back home.

"See... I'm fine," Darren said, stepping into the kitchen to his mother.

"I know love, we just worry that's all," Sarah said, giving him a hug. "So, did you enjoy your walk? Looks like the rain is coming back."

"Yeah it was nice. I think I'll go watch some television," Darren replied.

For the remainder of the day he sat staring at the screen watching the meaningless images flick passed one another.

The family shared their evening dinner together as usual, later, William and Sarah went upstairs to bed leaving Darren downstairs.

Once happy that both his parents were sound asleep, Darren rolled up the sleeve on his right arm and pulled the plasters off the wound he had inflicted on himself. Some blood had seeped from it onto the plasters and the cut was slightly open displaying the bright flesh beneath it. He moved the wound closer to his face and examined it further. *What is missing? Why can't I feel you?* He thought to himself.

Not wanting the wound to reopen fully and to help prevent infection, he stepped into the kitchen and closed the door behind him. He found a spoon in the drawer, lit the gas cooker and held the spoon above the bright blue flames. Once satisfied the utensil was hot enough, he held his right arm outright and immediately pressed the spoon hard against his skin in order to cauterise the cut. He wondered what affect the act would have on him if he could feel the hot implement but alas there was nothing.

Happy the injury had been treated, Darren washed the spoon, dried it fully and placed it back into the drawer. He returned to the sitting room, forgetting to switch off the cooker before doing so. He lowered himself back down onto the cosy sofa and began to channel hop, eventually the flickering images in front of him became hypnotising and he drifted off to sleep.

Meanwhile the plastic handle on one of the saucepans left resting on the opposite ring on the cooker began to melt due to the continuous, high temperature. As the handle drooped and got closer to the flames it began to liquefy. It didn't take long for the plastic to flash ablaze, which quickly caused the tea towel beside the cooker to catch fire and then the plastic draining board by the sink. Within minutes, the kitchen was an uncontrollable inferno.

Before he knew what was happening, Darren was being dragged from the sofa, through the hallway and out through the forced open front door by one of the attending firemen. Two more were battling the blaze in the kitchen, and another was checking the upstairs rooms as best he could through the dense plumes of smoke.

"I've two more up here!" he, roared downstairs to the others.

Within seconds, he had his arms around William, and moments later his colleague had a firm hold of Sarah and they were removed from the tomb of smoke.

"What happened? Where are my parents?" Darren asked, still trying to gather himself outside, while taking in the sight of the intense puffs of smoke bellowing from the windows and beneath the roof of his home.

The fire officer looked at him blankly, as Darren scouted the area for any sign of his mother and father.

He turned and raced for the house realising that they must be still inside, however he was quickly restrained.

"Let me go. I have to save them!" Darren cried, trying to escape the grasp of the large man bear hugging him. "Why are you just standing here, get them out of there!"

An eternity passed until he witnessed his mother and father's limp bodies being carried from the building.

"Let me go, I have to make sure they are okay," Darren said, thrashing about in the fireman's firm grip.

The ambulance arrived shortly after the fire brigade and the paramedics raced to the elderly couple, to examine for any sign of life and work on preserving it. However, the couple had inhaled too much fumes and both were dead before they reached fresh air. Darren's only saving grace was the sitting room window which had been left slightly open earlier that evening, allowing the smoke to escape.

The fire had begun to burn its way into the sitting room before he was rescued and due to his condition, the heat had no effect on Darren, leaving him firmly within his slumber.

"What happened? Can I see them now?" Darren

asked, tiring under the restraint.

"Not yet, just let them help them. Is there anyone else in the house?" The fireman quizzed.

No response came, Darren just stared toward the blue lights flashing frantically on the roof of the ambulance his parents were being examined within.

"Hey, is there anyone else in the house?" the fireman asked again.

"No just us," Darren confirmed, sitting on the grass beneath him trying to calculate what was happening.

Sometime later, the last of the fire crew, turned off the hose, exited the house and signalled to the others he fire was out. By then a large group of people had gathered at the front wall due to all the commotion.

"Who called you?" Darren asked, looking up towards the fireman still watching over him.

"You neighbour across the way saw the smoke and rang."

"Could he not have banged on the window or something to wake me up before you got here?" Darren snapped. "I mean, I could have gotten my parents out and then tried to put it out."

The fireman didn't respond, he didn't want to get involved in any such argument.

When news finally broke that his parents had died from smoke inhalation, Darren was convinced he was still fast asleep. Although physical pain was alien to him, emotional pain was not. He felt time slow to a snail's pace, hearing the words repeat in his mind repeatedly that his parents were dead.

"Can I see them?" Darren asked, once the doctor revealed the heart-breaking words to him.

"You can, we need you to formally identify the bodies. Are you sure you are up to doing it now though?" The doctor asked, placing a hand on Darren's shoulder.

"Yeah, I'll be fine. I just need to see them," Darren said, standing to his feet, still wrestling with the thought that William and Sarah were gone.

"Okay, follow me," the doctor instructed.

Darren did as asked and was led through the long white corridors towards the morgue.

Once he saw the sign displaying the large six letters, highlighting the room which his parents were laying in, Darren paused. He couldn't believe he was about to get the visual confirmation that his parents were gone.

The doctor placed his hand on the cold steel door handle and turned to Darren, "You're sure? We can do it a little later if you wish."

"No, I'm fine, we'll do it now," Darren replied, taking a deep breath and stepping forward.

The doctor opened the door and walked inside, holding the door aside for Darren.

Stepping into the morgue, he was greeted by a huge room with bright lights, a wall of stainless-steel doors to the right and to the left sat a screen in front of two isolated trolleys.

"This way," the doctor said, holding his arm out toward the plastic barrier concealing William and Sarah.

When they reached the screen, the doctor checked one final time with Darren, then moved it to one side revealing two trollies with the outline of a body beneath a large white sheet on each one.

As respectfully as he could, the doctor stepped to the head of the first body, lifted and folded the sheet to expose William's face. He walked to the next body, and carried out the same process to reveal Sarah.

Darren nodded to indicate that they were the bodies of his mother and father.

"Did they feel anything?" Darren asked.

"No, they passed in their sleep due to smoke inhalation." was the reply.

"Can I have some time alone with them?" Darren asked.

"Of course," the doctor said with a gentle smile and left the room.

Hearing the door closing, Darren walked over to his mother and placed his hand gently against her cheek, "I'm so sorry. It's all my fault," he said, staring at his mother's closed eyes.

He turned to his father, who also looked as though he was in a peaceful slumber, "I fell asleep, I killed you both."

Darren stared at the bodies in front of him unbelievingly for some time then removed his hand from his mother's face, which he assumed to be cold, and placed the sheets back over each of the bodies.

He walked to the door, stopped, looked back towards his parents one last time and then left the room to begin dealing with life without them.

Being an only child and having little family due to William and Sarah's siblings being deceased, meant that Darren only had a few scattered, estranged cousins, so he would have to organise the funerals of his beloved parents himself. Another aspect of the aftermath Darren had to consider was where he was going to spend the night, because his home had suffered extensive smoke and fire damage. Luckily, he did have some funds he had saved over the years in the bank so it would be possible to get by for a while.

Chapter 3

Following the funerals, it took some time for the life insurance to come through. However, what Darren didn't know was that his parents had willed all their life savings to him. This gave him the means to pay for the burials, repair the house and put it on the market. Although it was his childhood home, he couldn't bring himself to live in a building where his parents died due to something he blamed himself for.

Instead he moved several miles away, into a small cottage in the countryside on the outskirts of town. His new home sat at the top of an old country laneway, surrounded by woodland, which was adjacent to one of the main routes into Arklow. With the move, Darren also purchased a small, black van, which had seen many miles over its lifetime, at a very good price. He didn't see the value in buying a brand new vehicle, he just needed something to get him to town and back, so it was the perfect purchase for him.

Arklow, a sizeable town, attracted a large number of tourists during the summer months and this year was no different. Many individuals, after spending some time browsing through the various quaint shops, would walk past Darren's property towards the golden, long beach a short distance away.

The first number of weeks after lowering his parents into the ground, Darren didn't step outside the house much and his only human interaction was with the family solicitor who had him finalise some paperwork with his signature, after that, he was left to himself to try and move forward as best he could with his life.

Experiencing the death of his parents and moving into a new home to begin building a new life didn't alleviate his interest in the inability to experience physical pain. In fact, grieving for William and Sarah, combined with now living alone, without any supervision in place, his obsession grew further.

There was something so strange about watching his skin slice open and the blood pour from it without a single internal effect which intrigued Darren. He hated himself for causing the fire that killed his parents and would give anything to have them back.

He often sat in darkness with a knife in his left hand, digging the blade into the flesh on his left forearm, viewing it as a form of punishment, even though he couldn't feel it, he could horribly scar himself for the stupidity he displayed the night William and Sarah died.

It was a beautiful Saturday afternoon as the sun weaved its glorious light through the heavy trees opposite Darren's home. As with all recent weekends, due to the fantastic summer sunshine, Arklow was heaving with visitors from around the country.

Darren sat in a large chair in the sitting room. Over the last several days the loss of his parents had really began to weigh on him, so much so that he couldn't bear to look at his reflection in the mirror when he awoke from the minimal sleep he gained each night.

I should have gone back inside and saved them, Darren thought to himself, daydreaming towards the window, *it should be me buried, not them.*

The sudden glint of the sharp blade beside him caught his eye, *I can't believe I let this happen.* Darren picked up the knife sitting on the arm of the chair. Over the last hour or so he had been contemplating how he could display the internal, emotional hurt he was going through and how much he hated himself. He was unable to look at himself anymore and decided the best way to move forward was to cut away the face that was always staring back at him.

He placed the edge of the blade against his left cheek and picked up the handheld mirror he had placed beside him from earlier that morning. Staring at himself, he pushed on the handle when suddenly there was a loud crash in the distance.

Darren dropped the knife and stepped outside to see what had caused the heavy thud.

Eyeing nothing, he began to make his way down his long driveway towards the road. Moments later, he discovered a car had been introduced to a telegraph pole just outside the entrance to his property. Stepping out passed the gate, Darren witnessed a woman sitting in the driver's seat, still dazed from the impact of smashing her face against the steering wheel.

Darren looked around quickly to see no one else coming to her aid and ran to the car.

"You okay?" Darren asked, opening the door beside her.

"My leg," she replied, wincing as she tried to move it.

Looking downward, Darren saw a bone protruding through her pants, resting against the thick plastic beneath the dash.

Darren studied her as he witnessed the agony pulsate through her body with each passing second.

"How does it feel?" Darren asked, staring at her facial expressions.

"What? Get help," the woman groaned, her leg saturated in blood.

This plea fell on deaf ears as Darren turned his attention back to the wound creating the woman's distress. He reached out and touched the lacerated flesh around the bone which caused the woman to scream louder, however it didn't deter him in the slightest. Darren reached into the vehicle once again and wrapped his fingers around the bone on display and slowly moved it to one side as the woman trashed about in agony as Darren once again examined her erratic response to something he had never felt.

"Did you call for help?" a voice asked from behind.

This snapped Darren's attention, and he quickly

answered with, "No, I am trying to stop the bleeding, do have you a phone?"

Within moments the emergency services where called and on route. Meanwhile Darren savoured the reaction he had witnessed whilst the man who had driven up on the accident kept the old woman as comfortable as he possibly could.

It was discovered that the woman had swerved to avoid a dog on the road, which caused the crash. She was taken to hospital and the Gardaí didn't need to question Darren as he didn't witness the accident happen.

Later that night Darren sat in his sitting room in complete darkness, he couldn't get the old woman's grimaces out of his mind. *What was she going through? How did it feel to have a snapped bone bursting out through her skin?* He repeatedly thought to himself as he dissected his reflection on the recent incident.

When his parents were alive, they were a welcome distraction, for the most part, to his increasing fascination with the inability to experience pain. Being around them meant that other things would grab his attention from time to time, but now that they were dead, there was nothing controlling the obsession consuming him.

Darren had to know first-hand how the feelings generated by physical pain caused the reactions he had seen earlier during the day. He decided the only way he would be able to satisfy his intrigue was to create a situation where someone was feeling immense agony so he could study each reaction no matter how minimal.

Chapter 4

The sun was bowing below the beautiful countryside as Darren finished washing up after his dinner.

Living alone meant that he had to leave the house a lot more to get groceries, it also meant he was beginning to meet quite a few more people during his time outside the walls which entombed his hours of obsessing and contemplating.

Over the last several days, while in town, Darren would bump into Mary, an elderly woman who lived alone a short distance from his house. She had a sweet, gentle smile and always said hello each time he met her. He often offered her a lift home, but she would politely decline, saying that she loved being out in the fresh air.

Darren assumed that she had to be in her mid-seventies and she was the perfect individual to carry out his study on. There would be little fight and, in his opinion, she was close to death either way so the benefits of experiencing pain through her outweighed the negatives.

Darren dried his hands after emptying the water from the sink and glanced outside to see the darkness slowly swallow his house. Before rolling his sleeves back down, he briefly looked at the scars on his arms which never had any impact on him. He considered that it would be a good way to start, to witness how a person reacted to the same type of injuries he had encountered himself.

Satisfied the time was right, Darren left his home, and made his way into the adjoining field. It was the best and simplest way to get to Mary's home without being seen, and the glow from the street lights in the not too distant town and bright moon overhead meant he could navigate his route with relative ease.

Stepping his way through the long grass, countless thoughts entered Darren's mind. He wondered what reactions he could create from inflicting pain on Mary and what descriptions she would provide to him. Would she scream? Would she cry? Would she grit her teeth? Would she pass out? These were just a few questions which excited him.

When he reached the back of Mary's tiny cottage the first thing he noticed was that the kitchen light was switched off. The second thing he spotted was the low hedge line to his right which would make it easy for him to gain access to the back yard before him. To Darren he didn't see what he was about to do as wrong, in fact the excitement and intrigue was almost unbearable.

Standing in silence, he peered towards the house and checked each window which was visible to him, satisfied he wouldn't be seen climbing into the yard, he made his move, careful to remain as quiet as possible as he did so, while checking on the house for any sign of Mary as he moved forward.

Once safely in the back garden, Darren eyed the top of one of the windows was open, obviously left that way due to the warm temperatures the area had been experiencing recently. He crouched down, removed his boots, as he didn't want to leave any heavy footprints and began slowly making his way towards the kitchen door. When he reached it, Darren tried the handle with a gloved hand and as he expected, it didn't budge.

He moved over to one of the dark windows and peeked inside to see the flickering television light making its way past a partially open door, he could also hear the sound being emitted from it.

Darren stood upright and turned his attention to the open window above him. With a quick leap he was on the window sill and pulled open the small piece of glass as far as he could. He reached in and down towards the handle below it. Darren unlatched the bigger window and slowly pulled it open.

He climbed into the kitchen, being sure to reclose the window behind him. Judging by the volume of the television, Darren assumed that Mary must be hard of hearing, but it also meant that his break-in had, so far, gone unnoticed. As he looked around the room, he noticed the items on the draining board beside the sink and one which caught his attention was the large steak knife glinting in the twinkling light. Darren fetched it and made his way towards the door in front of him.

Peeking through the crack in the doorway, Darren

paused to see Mary sleeping comfortably in an armchair in front of the television. He double checked the room as much as he could before stepping inside to ensure she was alone, although he had learned that she was the only person who lived in the house, he had to be sure.

He gently pushed open the door, praying it wouldn't creak in the process to wake Mary, giving away his presence, before he got close enough to her.

Stepping through the room he noted the vast amount of black and white pictures covering the walls, each one displaying Mary's huge, contagious smile.

Reaching Mary, Darren stood over her for a moment taking in the sight before him. He studied every wrinkle, every strand of grey hair drifting down onto her shoulders and the jewellery she proudly displayed on her withered hands. He cast his attention back to the closed, crinkled eyelids and considered once again what he was about to do. Every reasoning in his mind was pointing to that he was doing the right thing, he had to know as best and as close as possible what pain felt like.

"Mary," Darren softly called, which caused her to shuffle about on the chair in front of him.

"Mary," Darren said a little louder.

Her eyes slowly opened and immediately widened seeing Darren looming over her in the room.

"Darren... what are you doing?" Mary asked, moving backward in the chair.

"I have to know how it feels, I'm sorry I just have to," Darren replied, taking one step forward.

It was then Mary eyed the large knife at his side.

"You need to leave before you do something stupid! Put the knife down and go!" Mary said, with as much confidence as possible, even though she was rattling with fear.

"I can't," Darren responded.

Seeing the intensity in his eyes, Mary tried to lift herself from the chair, however old age meant that she was unable to do it fast enough to escape Darren's grasp.

Darren reached forward and pressed a firm hand on her shoulder, pushing her back against the chair. In a panic Mary reached for the closest thing to hand which was the remote control for the television. She swung it with all her might and struck him above his left eye brow, which had absolutely no effect on him. She struck him once again as hard as possible. Smiling, Darren slapped the remote from her hand and then raised the knife to her throat.

"You do anything like that again and I'll push this in one side and out the other, you understand?" Darren said, glaring down at her.

"Okay... okay, I'm sorry," Mary stuttered, trying to calm him somewhat.

"Now raise your right arm," Darren instructed.

"What?" Mary asked, still in shock with what was happening to her.

"Just do it and don't ask any questions," Darren

said, raising his voice as he pressed the blade a little harder to her fragile neck.

Mary did as she was told. Meanwhile Darren lifted his right knee and placed his body weight firmly onto Mary's legs on the chair to ensure she was unable to escape, taking note of her deep inhale as he did it.

"Roll up the sleeve and don't try anything. I just want to know what it feels like!" Darren said with an unblinking gaze towards her.

Confused by the comment, Mary did exactly that without any question.

Darren took hold of the bare arm and examined every freckle, every hair and every crease. He removed the edge of the blade from her throat and placed the tip gently against the shrivelled skin covering Mary's limb, as her heart beat rapidly. He softly pulled the knife towards him as he watched the edge of it bounce along her flesh, creating a subtle crimson line on her arm behind it.

Mary considered screaming for her life, but she knew that it would do no good as the closest neighbour was quite a distance away and she was sure that Darren would plunge the blade into her if she did.

"Please don't," Mary begged.

There was no reply, instead Darren pressed the tip harder against the defenceless woman's arm and began once again to pull the blade towards him.

This action caused Mary to retract in pain.

"What does it feel like?" Darren asked, turning

towards her.

"What?" Mary asked, her breathing growing heavier with each passing second.

"Just tell me what it feels like!" Darren snapped towards her.

"I... I don't know, sore," Mary responded.

"Describe it to me in every detail, why does it cause you to wince like that?" Darren asked, as he pointed the knife to her face.

"It just does, I don't know what you want me to say. Please stop this," Mary pleaded.

This answer wasn't enough, Darren needed to know what feelings she was experiencing and decided that he needed to go further.

Without warning Darren forced the blade deep into Mary's arm and pulled the knife slowly down her forearm which caused her to scream in agony as Darren analysed her reaction. He removed the blade and sank it into her again, this time the blade ricocheted off the bone within the thin limb in the process. Mary writhed about in front of him as he watched the flesh split either side of the steel, while the blood poured from it and pooled on the floor beneath them.

"Can you feel each cut?" Darren asked.

Mary couldn't reply, she reached for the blade however Darren delivered a rapid, firm punch to her face dazing her instantly.

Unsatisfied with the information he had gathered so far, Darren grabbed Mary by the throat and placed the knife against her forehead, he punctured the skin and dragged the knife from left to right, as the blood saturated her face, legs kicking uncontrollably in anguish as he did so.

"Tell me everything. I want to know what you are going through," Darren instructed.

Screams were the only response he received, which added to his rising frustration.

"Useless!" Darren exhaled and stood upright, releasing the pressure on his old victim's weak body.

Mary slumped over in the chair as Darren looked towards the blood-soaked knife in his hand. He gripped the handle tighter and slammed the blade into Mary's tiny thigh, which caused her to rattle back to life and roar for help.

"All I wanted to know was what it felt like, but you are no benefit to me at all. You're too busy experiencing something I can't. You know what happens to things that are useless? They are disposed of," Darren said, putting the edge of the blade back to Mary's neck once more.

Looking deep into her eyes, Darren pushed on the handle and then slit the old woman's throat.

As he watched her gurgle for air with widened eyes, Darren envied her somewhat, she would die while experiencing the most intense feeling she had probably ever experienced.

When he was confident Mary was dead, Darren examined the wounds which caused her death. He pulled open the cuts on her forearm to reveal the bright tissue and bone underneath. *Looks exactly like mine,* Darren thought, in relation to the injuries he had previously inflicted upon himself. In a sense, he hoped he would get a physical answer or confirmation to why he was so different to everyone else, but he knew he wouldn't obtain it now.

Placing a palm on her forehead he raised her head to reveal the laceration in her throat, again he studied it for a moment and then released her head, to flop back into its original position.

The night had been a failure. Darren wanted answers but the only results was a slashed old body in front of him.

Darren knew he couldn't leave her body on display as it was, so he returned to the kitchen he had accessed the house from. He didn't turn on the light as he wanted to leave everything as it was as much as possible and used the illumination from the sitting room to search the many drawers he was greeted with. He quickly retrieved a lighter and moved back to the sitting room.

The television program Mary had been watching before falling asleep was just finishing as he stood in front of the limp body, blood still trickling from it to the carpet below.

Darren flicked the lighter to life and lowered the flame towards the dressing gown covering Mary's tiny frame. He watched the material singe and finally catch fire. Not content with this being the only source, he held the lighter to the heavy curtains covering the sitting room window.

When he turned back to Mary's body, it was sitting in a growing blaze, her skin becoming more charred with each passing second. In his mind Darren could still hear her screams due to the wounds he had inflicted on her and was sure, if alive, she would be emitting the same sounds from within the flames.

Confident that the house would soon be swallowed by fire, Darren made his way back to the kitchen, ensuring to close over the door back into its original position before he broke into the house. He washed the knife thoroughly, then bleached it and the sink. He was confident the flames would destroy all evidence, however he wanted to make sure he covered himself as much as possible. After this he reopened the kitchen window, climbed through it and was sure to latch it back into position so that it wouldn't be completely obvious that someone had broken in. Before making his way to the fields which he had used to get to Mary's house, Darren turned to witness the flames beginning to dance their way past the door he just used. He quickly made his way back over the ditch, laced up his boots, turned right and walked towards home.

During his journey the frustration continued to bubble within him. Although he had observed and heard the impact of the hurt he had caused on another person, he still was none the wiser to what it felt like.

Reaching home, Darren removed his clothing, the

disposable gloves and placed them all into a large bin bag. He then lit the fire in the sitting room and waited until it became suitable to dispose of the evidence. He added the bag to the flames and then placed further coal on top of it to ensure the temperature would stay constant for quite a long time.

Hearing a car pass by in the distance outside, he was happy that he had used the fields to cover his movements, because if he had been seen walking the road, he was sure he would instantly be a person of interest. However, Darren was sure that he had carried out his experiment leaving no trace behind.

Darren then went to the bathroom and got a shower. Once finished he lay on his bed staring at the ceiling above him listening to the sirens wailing in the distance. He was sure by then that Mary's body would be burnt beyond anyone noticing the wounds, the primary cause he wanted everyone to assume was that the fire caused her death.

Although he had carried out a heinous act, Darren didn't see it as such, to him he looked at it as a way of living through others. He decided he would have to select the correct people around him to do this, it would be his connection to something he could never have.

He rubbed his forehead where Mary had struck him and reminded himself to check it for any bruising the following morning, as even a trivial thing may cause suspicion.

Turning to his side Darren felt, all things

considered, somewhat content for the first time in quite some time. He had spent so long trying to self-inflict the impossible hurt, however now he had a route to the closest way in which he could, and that was through other people's suffering.

As Darren drifted off to a sound sleep, the local fire brigade was beginning to gain control on the fire which had ravaged the cottage and the old woman's body which had been butchered and unceremoniously abandoned within it.

Darren's unmanaged obsession had consumed him and there was now only one way which he could feed his fascination, torture people so much they would have to reveal the answers he needed.

Chapter 5

Darren awoke the following morning to the sounds of birds chirping and dancing happily among one another upon the roof of his house. Turning, he could see the bright sunshine colliding against the bedroom curtains. He paused a moment and thought of the act he had carried out the night before. No remorse crashed over him, just a growing obsession to examine people's reactions further.

He swung around on the mattress, lifted himself and walked over to the bedroom window. He pulled back the curtains to reveal a beautiful, glowing day outside. His actions caused the birds overhead to flutter away quickly, just like any thoughts he may have had that what he did the previous night was wrong.

Darren got dressed and went to the bathroom to have a shave. He applied the shaving cream to his thin face and began the process. He remembered when his father taught him how to shave. William would stand and watch over him for the first number of months to ensure Darren didn't seriously injure himself. "Keep an eye on your skin and the pressure you put on it, if you see any bleeding, stop straight away," Darren remembered his father instructing him. Over the years he eventually became familiar of how to read his skin's reaction to the pressure of the blade on his face and the colour his flesh would turn if he applied too much force upon it.

After shaving, Darren checked his forehead once more and was thankful no bruising had developed after Mary's attempt to save herself.

He had his breakfast, collected his keys, got into his van, and made his way towards town.

It didn't take long for him to notice the small group of people gathered outside Mary's front gate, shocked at the charred scene in front of them.

"What happened?" Darren asked, as he pulled over to the side of the road.

"I don't know, but Mary unfortunately was in there last night," Joseph, a neighbour living closer to town, replied.

"You mean she's dead?" Darren asked, displaying his best, fake, shocked face as he stared towards the smouldering ruins.

"I'm afraid so, we heard about it earlier this morning. How have you been doing? I was so sorry to hear about your parents. Two fires in such a small period is shocking," Joseph continued.

It haven't crossed Darren's mind about the time scale between the two house fires, however he was convinced he had done enough to cover his tracks.

"I'm doing okay thanks... just taking it all as it comes. Was Mary the only person in there?" Darren asked, turning the conversation back to the incident at hand.

"Yes. She lived alone," Joseph said.

"It's so frightening how easy these things happen. I still hate myself for forgetting about the cooker, I could have prevented their deaths, but instead I was asleep on the couch while they both suffocated in the room above me," Darren exhaled, shaking his head, staring blankly at the dash in front of him.

"I'm sorry, I didn't mean to bring up any bad memories," Joseph said, resting a hand on the young man's shoulder.

"It's okay. I hope Mary didn't suffer," Darren returned, knowing in his mind that she had greatly, by his hand.

"Yeah, me too," Joseph replied, before Darren said goodbye and continued driving towards town.

While making his way to the hardware shop, Darren began to think of how he could keep carrying out what he started with Mary without getting caught and one solution he came up with more than once, was to target people who visited their holiday homes in the holiday park beside the beach. Many people would visit from different counties around the country and the nicer the weather, the more people the town would attract. Darren rationalised that it would take someone's family a lot longer to know that they were missing if they were holiday makers, rather than someone disappearing from the town.

He would have to calculate if it was best to strike within the park or wait somewhere outside it to make his move. Either way, Darren just had to know how a person felt when he sliced into and tortured them many different ways.

Reaching the local hardware shop, Darren made his way to the tool section and right on cue he was asked if he needed help with anything by staff member, to which his quick answer was, "No."

He browsed the numerous snips and hammers on display, and selected one of each, picked up some duct tape and went to the counter to pay for them.

"Terrible what happened out the road isn't it?" The shopkeeper said, as she rang up the till.

"Yeah, I just drove by it, there is hardly anything left," Darren said, as he took hold of the bag as she handed it to him.

"Thank you."

"Thanks, see you later," Darren replied and left the shop.

Darren considered purchasing cable ties and some other items too, but he thought it a little stereotypical for what he wanted the objects for, he may as well have added a balaclava and a chainsaw to the order to really put a spotlight on him he grinned to himself as he made his way back home.

Passing by Mary's home once more, Darren didn't look towards it, in his opinion she was insignificant and in the past. It was important to him to plan the next sensory experiment, however he had to wait for the cover of darkness to begin selecting the next participant to help him better understand what it meant to be normal.

Night had descended as Darren doubled checked the locks to his house. He walked to the end of his driveway, secured the gate behind him, and made his way towards the holiday park. Excitement built within as he thought about who he was going to select to help him better understand what he was missing.

He decided to walk instead of driving because someone may recognise his van if he parked it outside when he was scouting for his next victim, and he could quickly leap into the ditch and hide when needed if anyone approached.

It didn't take long for him to reach the chain-link fence at the border of the site. He was greeted with silence. Any families who had young children had settled down for the night, and there were only a few remaining scattered lights twinkling about the area.

Ensuring no one was near, Darren gripped the fence and climbed his way over it, being sure to create as little noise as possible.

Once on the other side, Darren slowly made his way over to one of the small mobile homes which was still illuminated from the inside, situated close to the fence he had just climbed past. Thankfully, the mobile home adjacent to the one he was stalking, was in complete darkness, indicating that the people within it were in a sound slumber.

Darren moved around to the side and was greeted by a brand new car and a clothesline full of designer clothing, some items of which would cost more than what he would spend on food for a week. He crept his way over to the window at the side of the home and peered inside to see a couple enjoying some drinks together.

Darren allowed some time to pass to ensure it was just the pair staying there and was satisfied they were the only occupants. Judging by what he saw, there didn't seem to be any children with them. *Perfect,* he thought to himself, rationalising that he would get two for the price of one. However, he wouldn't strike just yet, he would have to put a little more planning into what he was going to do, he couldn't carry out his examinations on them inside the mobile home because it surely would attract attention. No, he would have to get them back to his house so he could experience and savour their pain in peace.

He retreated from the oblivious couple and carefully made his way back home. As he did, he could visualise their faces contorted in agony, highlighting what they were going through, which brought a huge smile to Darren's face.

Climbing into bed, Darren's mind was swelling with various thoughts about how he was going to get his next victims safely back to his home, he knew he had to strike under the cover of darkness, but he had to ensure he got them both under his control at the same time. He would have to use his van to transport them together, rather than bringing them back one at a time, if he did it that way, there was a greater risk of getting caught.

The following morning Darren got dressed and stepped out into an overcast day. He decided to check out the area he was going to take his next victims from in better light, but in a way that wouldn't be too obvious or cause any suspicion.

Walking towards the holiday park, Darren glanced to the sky overhead and couldn't help but notice that one of the clouds above him resembled a humanlike face, screaming. He found this very assuming as a smirk cracked across his face.

Darren met a number of people, who greeted him with warming smiles and hellos, along the way which to him had both a positive and a negative impact on his plan. On the plus side it meant it would be very difficult for anyone to narrow it down to him who, stalked the couple due to the footfall in the area, however, it also meant he had to be extremely careful not to be seen taking the pair away from their second home in the holiday park.

Rounding the corner, Darren saw the fence he climbed over the previous night and the fancy mobile home housing the couple he had selected to help him better understand what it was like to experience pain.

He slowed his pace as his began to calculate the best way to execute the kidnapping. Darren noted that the mobile home was very near the fence and had a heavy treeline hanging over it, which made it a good position to take them from the site due to the cover it created. The road also widened at this location and there was an area where he could easily park his van close by. Continuing to slowly pass by the property, Darren took note of anything around the home which would impede his task. He observed a small barbeque to one side with two deck chairs beside it, he also witnessed the couple's neighbours placing packed bags into the back of their car, which lead him to believe that they were returning home.

"Even better," Darren said under his breath, knowing that it would make his job a little easier with the less people around.

Darren walked beyond the park and continued some distance up the road as not to cause any suspicion about his movements.

On his way back home, he eyed the departing family drive past him, one of their young children waving to him from the back window of the car as they did.

Next, Darren had to decide how he would restrain the couple while transporting them. He opened the huge steel door to the shed at the back of his house, many of the items within had been left behind by the previous owners. He found some rope and left it to one side while he cleared some floor space around the two thick steel pillars rising from the floor, supporting the roof. He paused a moment, realising that he couldn't just spill their blood willy-nilly around his property, he would have to contain as best he could in some way.

Darren stepped to his kitchen, retrieved the large bin bags from beneath the sink, returned to the shed and began taping them to the floor underneath him as his eagerness grew each passing moment. Happy with the preparation, he left and locked the door.

Darren made himself dinner and then watched television as he waited for nightfall. He noticed a fog beginning to blanket the countryside which helped him make the decision that night was the perfect opportunity because it would disguise his movements further.

He looked towards the clock on the mantelpiece to see it was just after midnight. Darren stood, went to his bedroom and dressed in dark clothing and a hoodie to cover his head. He pulled two disposable gloves from the box he kept in the kitchen and went outside. He fetched a screwdriver from the back of his van, removed the registration plates from the vehicle and placed them beside the house. He double checked his supplies – hammer, snips, rope and duct tape, then climbed into the van and made his way to the entrance to his property. Closing the gate behind him, Darren momentarily took note of the dead silence around him and reconfirmed in his mind this was the best time to take the couple from the safety of their property.

As he made his way towards the holiday park, the fog seemed to become thicker and thicker, so much so that he thought he was going to have to stop to let it pass. However, Darren was determined to get the job done.

When he arrived at his destination, he parked the

van as close to the fence as possible to make it easier to get the targeted individuals into it and it also wouldn't be blatantly obvious to any random passer-by. Darren turned off the engine and stepped out of the vehicle, being sure to leave the door open, gently shutting it over behind him before it latched into place. He got the snips and began cutting up through the fence protecting the area. He placed the tool into his pocket and retrieved the rope and hammer from the van. Pressing the door softly shut, Darren then made his way through the fence, the blanket of fog swaying elegantly around him in the gentle breeze.

Unlike the night previously, all the lights in the mobile home were off and Darren could hear the snores echoing from inside. He approached the door and tried the handle. It didn't budge.

He knew he would have to strike fast for his plan to work.

Darren began to subtlety knock on the glass door in front of him with his right hand, while gripping the hammer tightly in his left. Although there were no neighbours staying close by, he still needed to be quiet and figured this was the best possible way to access his victims rather than trying to break into their mobile home.

Moments later the snoring stopped and there was movement from inside. Darren stopped tapping his knuckles against the glass and waited whilst he observed one of the internal lights flick to life. He crouched lower beside the door when he witnessed a silhouette behind it and hearing the lock disengage.

"Hello?" came the man's voice, wondering who was visiting at such a late hour.

Darren suddenly pounced, delivering a vicious blow to the man's abdomen with the head of the hammer, which caused the wind to instantly leave his body as he hunched over in pain gasping for air. Darren stopped in his tracks to study the reaction, but quickly reminded himself that now was not the time.

Turning the hammer upright and with one powerful downward blow, he introduced the end of the handle to the back of the man's head, knocking him unconscious.

"Brendan?" A female voice called from the bedroom. However, he was lying face down in the doorway.

Darren passed by him, grabbed Brendan's ankles tightly and dragged him back inside, being sure to close the door in the process.

"Everything okay? Who was at the door?" The woman asked from behind the partially opened door at the opposite side of the room.

Darren quickly placed a thick piece of duct tape over Brendan's mouth and then rapidly secured his wrists behind his back with rope, finishing by firmly tying his ankles together.

Hearing the bedroom door open, Darren spun and witnessed a shocked woman staring at the horrifying scene before her.

"Oh my God," she stuttered, her eyes staring in

disbelief.

Darren darted for her as she tried to close and lock the door. Before the latch was engaged, Darren slammed his shoulder hard against the feeble door, causing it to swing forcefully open, throwing the tiny woman onto the mattress in the process.

"Help," she screamed, as Darren leapt on top of her and covered her mouth to prevent any further calls for aid escaping her.

"I just want to know what it feels like, that's all," Darren said, staring deep into the terrified woman's eyes.

In retaliation she began to slap and punch Darren as hard as she could, which had absolutely no effect on him.

"Stop it!" Darren instructed, wrapping his free hand around her throat to hold her in position.

However, she continued to flight for her life as much as she could.

"I said stop!" Darren yelled, raising his voice more than he desired to. He needed to be fast and create very little commotion.

Wanting to cease the racket quickly, Darren clenched his fist and drove it hard against the woman's temple. Her struggle slowed but in her dazed state, she continued to fight. This caused Darren to rain down another vicious blow to her head, immediately knocking her out.

He didn't waste any time securing her mouth and then her limbs, so she, like Brendan, could be transported to the van as easily and quietly as possible.

Darren stood and eyed his reflection in the mirror opposite the bed in the tiny bedroom. Before him he saw a man who was determined to know what it felt like to be the same as everyone else and was certain what he was doing was within his rights.

Darren turned off all the lights within the mobile home and then made sure that all the curtains were pulled across all windows. While carrying out the task, he was sure no traffic had passed by on the road, however, with all the commotion, he could not be certain.

He dragged the woman's limp body over and lay her beside Brendan.

Darren reached for the curtain on the window beside the door and peeked outside to check that the route was clear to the fence line he had cut his way through. Seeing it was, Darren slowly opened the door, stepped out into the night and turned back towards the mobile home. He grabbed Brendan and pulled him towards the steps and then hauled him up onto his shoulder.

Darren moved towards his van as fast as his legs could carry him, being sure not to get any parts of his clothes caught on the wire fence on the way through it as he did and laid the limp body into the back of the van. He swiftly returned to the mobile home, collected the woman's body and placed her into the back of the van also.

Before he drove away from the scene, Darren was sure to close the door on the home he had just dragged his victims from and then made his way over to the fence. Stepping through it, he then pulled the two separated sides back together and wrapped the cut pieces of wire around one another to create the illusion of the fence being unaltered.

Darren jumped into the driver's seat, started the engine and made his way back home.

During the drive, Darren hoped he wouldn't meet anyone along the journey and was thankful to reach the gate to his property hindrance free. He opened and then closed the gate quickly behind him, then breathed a sigh of relief when he witnessed the headlights of a passing vehicle in his rear-view mirror as he drove up the driveway to his house, happy that whoever it was hadn't seen him.

Darren reversed and parked the van in front of the door to the shed he had prepared for his subjects.

He carried both individuals from the van and attached them firmly to the pillars in the centre of the shed via a chain around their waists and necks.

Tired and rationalising that his victims wouldn't be fully coherent for some time after the ordeal, Darren double checked the duct tape covering their mouths and their restraints. Before leaving the shed, he made sure that there was nothing close to them which could help them escape when they came to. Happy, Darren placed a heavy blanket over the pair, due to them still being in their underwear, turned off the light and locked the door securely behind him.

Climbing into bed, a smile crept across Darren's face, he couldn't wait until morning to begin his next examinations.

Chapter 6

Darren awoke the following morning and leapt from the bed with excitement. He quickly dressed, had some breakfast and stepped out into a bright, warm summer's day.

Darren paused momentarily, taking in his peaceful surroundings.

He turned and made his way towards the shed where he was keeping the young couple he kidnapped.

Swinging open the door, Darren saw the pair slumped over in the same position he had left them.

Hearing the door open, Brendan slowly opened his eyes, looked towards Darren, then towards his girlfriend tied and shackled beside him.

"Don't worry, I didn't kill her," Darren said, grinning to him.

This caused Brendan to erupt into a tirade of shuffling about on the floor and unconceivable mumblings.

"Oh, you don't believe me?" Darren joked, "I'll show you," he said, reaching for a pliers sitting on the work bench to his left.

Darren made his way over to the helpless woman in front of him, as Brendan did his utmost to break free from the chains and rope holding him in place.

Darren reached down, grabbed the woman's, bound left hand and held out her index finger. Without hesitation, he placed her fingernail between the jaws of the pliers and clamped down on it firmly. Darren turned to Brendan and slowly began to pull the fingernail upward.

This motion and injection of pain caused the woman to jump to consciousness, her mind bombarded by the unfamiliar surroundings, not being able to move or talk, but most of all the growing excruciating agony pulsing from her fingernail being steadily torn from her finger.

She began to writhe about uncontrollably as the tears trickled down her cheeks and over the tape covering her mouth.

Darren stopped a moment and closed his eyes. Listening to the choir of pain and torment brought a sense of satisfaction, something he had never experienced. Looking towards the woman, he smiled once more and then with one quick, jolting motion he ripped off the fingernail, which caused her body to jump about violently as much as the restraints would allow

"You're doing so well," Darren said, concentrating on the agony projected from behind her mouth covering. He turned to Brendan, "I hope you are as good as she seems to be."

Darren stood and placed the pliers back onto the workbench, before turning and closing the door.

"I'm going to remove the gags one at a time and I

want you to tell me how it feels, every little detail," Darren said, looking towards the bewildered couple in front of him. "I know you will scream and shout when we start the process, but I need you to be specific for me. Concentrate on the pain, what you are going through and describe it."

To his right sat a bench with various tools and implements his father had collected over the years.

Darren turned his attention back to the woman who was still rattling from the injury he had inflicted on her.

"We'll continue with you," Darren said, walking back over and squatting down in front of her.

He reached forward and took hold of her chin, "I just want you to help me understand, that's all. I'm going to remove the tape. Screaming for help will do no good, no one will hear you!"

Pinching the edge of the duct tape, Darren slowly began to remove it, as it stretched and pulled on the skin behind it.

"Please," the woman instantly stuttered once her lips were free to do so, the blood still dripping from her nail-less finger. "You can stop now, and we won't tell anyone. Just let us go before you go too far."

"Too far?" Darren asked, eyebrows scrunched, venom in his words, "I'm just trying to understand, that's all."

Confusion crashed across the woman's face.

"What is your name?" Darren asked.

The woman paused a moment, still hoping she was

about to wake up from a cruel nightmare.

"Name?" Darren requested once again.

"Rebecca," she replied, glancing around the shed to see if there was any way to escape.

"Okay Rebecca, I need you to be strong okay? Help me understand," Darren instructed standing upright.

Deciding to start off light, Darren retrieved the pliers once more and reached for Rebecca's tied hands again. He placed the jaws of it around the nail on her left middle finger and squeezed.

"Please, please, please don't do this," Rebecca pleaded, as Brendan mumbled in protest beside her.

Without any hesitation Darren ripped the nail from the finger, causing Rebecca to erupt in pain again.

Darren dropped the pliers to the floor and placed his hands either side of her head, "Tell me what it is like?"

Rebecca recoiled and winced against the pillar she was fixed to.

"Did you hear me?" Darren asked, watching the tears pour down the anguish ridden face in front of him. "Hey, don't lose it now, just tell me how it feels," he continued.

These words had no effect on Rebecca, she was concentrating on dealing with the throbbing, bleeding wounds.

As he studied her, Darren could see the discomfort she was going through, but he needed more as his frustration increased.

"Snap out of it," Darren said, slapping her across the face, Brendan trying his hardest to break free so he could subject Darren to exactly what he was doing to them.

"HELP!" Rebecca roared, saliva spraying from her mouth.

"Focus," Darren instructed, slapping her harder.

Rebecca's torrents of tears continued, and the only response Darren received was the sobbing sounds filling the room.

Useless, Darren thought to himself, clenching his right fist tightly.

"So, you're not going to tell me?" the angered man asked.

Rebecca paid no attention to the question as she turned to look helplessly at Brendan.

Without any hesitation Darren introduced his fist to her face as hard as he possibly could, causing her head to rattle about and bounce off the thick pillar. He stood and watched Rebecca slump over as blood began to trickle from her mouth.

"She had potential, but I hope you are better than her!" Darren said, turning to Brendan.

He walked over to the bench and picked up a flathead screwdriver. Darren stepped to Brendan, who was still staring at his beautiful Rebecca who was viciously knocked unconscious again.

"I'm going to fucking kill you for this!" Brendan snarled, when Darren pulled the gag from his mouth.

"Come on, we don't need, nor have time for any empty threats," Darren grinned. "Now hold still."

Darren raised the edge of the screwdriver up to Brendan's left eye, Brendan shook his head from left to right with the tiny bit of space he had within the restraints in order to prevent Darren getting a good placement for the tool.

"If you don't stop moving it's going to be a lot worse," Darren said, grabbing Brendan's chin and holding it in position with his free hand.

However, Brendan continued to fight as best he could.

"Stop moving or I'll cut her throat right now in front of you!" Darren instructed.

"Do whatever you want to me, but leave her alone," Brendan replied, still in shock and succumbing to the threat to Rebecca's life.

"Look straight forward," Darren instructed, raising the screwdriver again.

He placed the cold steel against the lower eyelid of Brendan's left eye, causing the bound man's breaths to become heavier with each passing second. Darren then began to slowly push the steel inward which caused Brendan to uncontrollably squint and turn away.

"Hold still!" Darren yelled, repositioning the screwdriver in front of Brendan's eye.

However, Brendan's natural reaction kicked in again and he turned his head away involuntarily.

Realising his initial approach wouldn't work

correctly, Darren fetched a large strap from the work bench, wrapped it around Brendan's forehead and the pillar. With several forceful tugs, he tied it firmly in position, locking Brendan's head in place.

"Don't do this, I'll pay you whatever you want," Brendan pleaded.

"This isn't about money. It's about something much more than that and there is only one way I can achieve what I want to," Darren replied.

Satisfied that his captive couldn't move his head, Darren reassumed the position in front of him. He placed his thumb and index finger on the top and bottom eyelid, pulled them apart wider and then began to push the tip of the screwdriver into the eye socket.

Brendan roared as the steel slowly edged further and further inside him, Darren analysing his reaction.

"Tell me," Darren instructed, pulling the screwdriver back out.

"What?" Brendan cried, thoughts racing and senses overloaded.

"What it feels like when I do that to you!" Darren replied.

"I don't know. Cold. Pressure and pain," Brendan stuttered.

Finally, Darren had got someone to give him an answer, even though it was just a tiny snippet. He was confident that if he continued to examine the reactions he would decipher more information.

"Details... give me every little detail," Darren

commanded.

"I don't know what more you want from me, how do you expect me to describe exactly what it feels like?" Brendan spluttered, blood trickling from his face.

Without warning Darren jabbed the implement back into the man's eye socket, a little further than before, causing Brendan to bellow in anguish.

"Can you feel it inside your face?" Darren asked, "Does it feel like a part of you now?"

Darren removed the screwdriver and stepped over to the work bench as Brendan panted deeply, trying to keep his mind on anything but the current torture he was experiencing.

Somewhat happy with the preliminary result, Darren still wanted more. He wrapped his hand around a ballpeen hammer and returned to Brendan.

"Don't go passing out on me, we've more to do before that," Darren said, hitting Brendan's face with the back of his hand.

"Please... Please let us go. We won't tell anyone about you. We'll never come back here again," Brendan continued.

"You think I believe that? What would you say when people asked where you got these injuries? You must really think I'm stupid! Well I'm far from that," Darren said, as he swung the cold steal head of the hammer, hard against Brendan's shoulder, resulting in a loud cracking sound.

Darren kept a close eye on him as the restrained

man gritted his teeth and rattled about on the floor.

"So?" Darren asked.

"I think you've dislocated it. Feels like my shoulder is twice the size and it's throbbing," Brendan replied, not able to decide which hurt more, his eye or his shoulder.

Darren reached forward and pulled aside the blanket to reveal a bruised lump, swelling more by the minute.

"You're sick you know that?" Brendan spat.

"What did you say?" Darren said, grabbing the helpless man by the neck.

"YOU'RE SICK IN THE HEAD!" Brendan howled. "If I wasn't tied up like this, you'd be the one calling for help."

"Oh really?" Darren laughed, as he began to undo the rope and chains holding Brendan in place and then stood in front of him. "Go on then, show me how I'm going to beg for help," Darren grinned.

Not caring that he only had one working eye and arm, Brendan lumbered himself upright in front of the man who had kidnapped and inflicted so much pain on him and his girlfriend.

"I'm going to kill you for hurting her," Brendan said, swiping his right fist wildly at Darren.

"Come on you can do better than that," Darren laughed, watching the man's feeble attempt swing past his face. "Try harder."

Brendan swung his fist once more catching Darren on the temple, causing him to laugh even louder.

"I'll give you one more chance before I tie you back up, try it with this, as hard as you can right here" Darren instructed, handing Brendan the hammer, lifting his hoodie to reveal his stomach.

Brendan didn't have to be asked twice and swung as hard as he could into Darren's abdomen, which didn't cause any reaction. Brendan stood in disbelief knowing that surely the blow he delivered should have grounded him.

"I'm sick in the head?" Darren asked, slapping the hammer from Brendan's hand. "You know nothing about what I go through, how much I want to be normal. But you're going to help me, even if you don't want to."

Brendan tried to dart for the shed door, however Darren reacted quickly, wrapping his arm around his chest, forced his thumb into the already damaged eye, pulled him to the ground and dragged him back over to the pillar, tying him back securely into position beside Rebecca.

"You don't know what you have, I'd give anything to feel like you do," Darren said showing the mark on his stomach left by the hammer.

Brendan didn't respond, as he began to cry, realising he was facing a situation he couldn't get out of.

"I'll let you both regather your strength before we continue," Darren said, walking back towards the door and firmly locking it behind him.

Outside Darren glanced towards his hands which

were covered in the residue of his captive's body fluids. He decided to go get a shower before going into town in order to maintain normal interaction with the community to prevent any suspicion arising around him.

Later, climbing into the van, Darren looked towards the shed where Brendan and Rebecca were held, wondering to himself what other procedures he could carry out on them to continue working toward the results he so much desired. Taking a break, also meant he could gather some head space to ensure he was covering his vicious activities correctly. Although he felt what he was doing was right, he knew nobody, only him would understand his reasoning behind it.

"Afternoon," the shopkeeper said, as Darren placed some small food items on the counter. "Beautiful day out there isn't it," she continued as she ran them through the till.

"It sure is, I think it's meant to last a while too," Darren smiled.

"Let's hope so, although then we'll be complaining of the heat," the shopkeeper laughed, handing over the small bag to Darren, who couldn't get is mind off returning home to enact the next sensory study session.

Walking back to his van, Darren's mind shot to his parent's bodies buried a short distance away. He momentarily considered what they may think of his recent actions, however he quickly reminded himself that it needed to be done so he could understand more about himself and life.

Returning home, Darren's eyes widened, and his mouth sprung agape when he witnessed two women standing aside the gate to his property.

"Can I help you?" Darren barked, screeching the van to a halt and glancing about the area to check if anyone else was close by.

"Sorry?" One of the women responded, looking towards him after stretching her legs, using the pillar supporting his gate as an aid.

Turning his attention back to the pair in front of him, it was clear they had been jogging and they decided to rest and stretch at the entrance to his home. Darren was confident they wouldn't have heard any cries for help due to placing the gags back on his victims, however, the less people who were around his property the better and that was assuming they hadn't been nosy and wondered past the gate, onto the large piece of land beyond it.

"What are you doing there?" Darren replied.

"None of your business," came a smart response from the other woman.

"Well actually it is, I live here," Darren spat.

"Oh sorry, we didn't realise. I thought you were just some nosy creep," the young woman returned, turning red from embarrassment.

"It's okay, I thought you were trying to break in or something," Darren giggled, considering adding to his prisoner count, as he stepped to open the heavy gate to his property.

Walking towards the slender women, Darren was sure he could overcome them quite easily, however his thoughts were interrupted by the sound of an oncoming car, making it too risky for him to strike.

"No, we were just catching our breath. Sorry to bother you," the woman smiled.

"No need to apologise at all, take care," Darren responded as he watched the pair make their way down the road from him, unaware just how much danger they had been in.

Parking in front of the building housing his victims, Darren unlocked the door to find Brendan and Rebecca still in the bloodied positions he left them.

While he was away, Rebecca had recovered consciousness and began breathing rapidly upon seeing Darren step in through the door and locking it.

"Oh hello," Darren said, spotting her staring at him.

From the bag, Darren pulled a container of salt from the other meaningless groceries he had picked up in order to keep face in the community. He placed a sharp blade he found in the toolbox beside him into his pocket and made his way over to Brendan, whose unharmed eye watched Darren's every movement.

Darren squatted in front of him which initiated mumblings from behind the gag. Darren removed the tape to be greeted with further pleas to let them go.

"Save your energy for this," Darren said, waving the salt in front of Brendan's face.

He flicked open the lid and loosened the restraint around Brendan's neck. Darren then gripped Brendan's hair, tilted his head backwards and began pouring the salt over his bloodied, mutilated eye.

"Fuck!" Brendan roared, rattling about as the immense, stinging pain injected its way through him.

Darren released Brendan, stood upright and turned towards Rebecca. He pulled the blade from his pocket, the sharp edge glinting in the light cast from the single bulb overhead. Rebecca's breathing deepened watching him move closer to her.

"Leave her alone," Brendan managed to spurt past his dry, cracked lips.

Darren placed the tip of the knife beneath her beautiful, smooth jawline and looked towards Brendan as Rebecca began to sob uncontrollably behind the tape covering her mouth.

"Please stop," Brendan begged.

Darren smiled and Rebecca's eyes rapidly widened and burst with tears as he forced the point of the blade into her skin, the blood pouring instantly past either side of the steel. He removed the knife and then quickly stabbed the blade into another part of her neck, removed it again and carried out the same act in a third location beneath her face, the crimson fluid spouting wildly from each wound.

"I'll kill you for this," Brendan threatened, helplessly watching the love of his life being murdered.

"You see this is important, it's good you are going

through this emotional distress," Darren responded.

Darren turned back to Rebecca, ripped the sticky material away from Rebecca's mouth and ran the blade down the centre of her face as she spat blood, gurgling for life to stay within her. He then introduced the knife to her neck one final time and twisted the handle.

Darren sat back and watched her die slowly in front of him, while Brendan roared in grief in the background.

Darren didn't pay any attention to Brendan's distraction however, he analysed each pupil dilation, watched as her facial features became relaxed, her limbs fallings limp at her sides, and her breath... ceased.

Reaching forward, Darren examined the wounds he inflicted on the body.

"Keep your hands off her!" Brendan roared, the tears pouring down his face and the pain from his own injuries still flowing through him.

This instruction fell on deaf ears however as Darren rooted around within the sliced skin with his fingertips. He parted one knife wound and looked inside, to him the sight of the flesh and blood looked the exact same as his which he had seen so many times over the years. Even though it was not true, he often expected that his flesh or wounds would look completely different than other individuals, but that simply was not the case. He pulled the edge of the blade across the top of her forehead, creating further protests from Brendan. Moving the blade downwards on either side of the cut and then across once more, Darren removed the rectangular piece of skin.

"Amazing isn't it?" Darren said, holding the piece of Brendan's girlfriend in front of him.

Brendan tried to break from the restraints once more, but his attempts were in vain.

"She wasn't great at communicating and actually gave me more from the process when dying, however you were able to give me an insight. That's something we'll continue to work on," Darren said, placing the piece of skin on Brendan's forehead to use it as a stencil to carve a piece from the captured man. Brendan roared as much as his lungs would allow.

"See, the exact same," Darren said, holding the two pieces of flesh in front of Brendan. "And if I did the same to myself, it too would look alike."

The blood from the facial wounds poured down Brendan's face, his body trying to manage the many sources of torture being inflicted upon it.

"Now let's see what this does," Darren said, dropping the skin to the floor, reaching forward and taking hold of Brendan's left ear.

He placed the blade behind the ear and began to slice downward, Brendan bellowing out once again.

"Tell me," Darren instructed. "Tell me what it feels like right now."

"Fuck you," Brendan spat.

Darren grabbed his throat and immediately began to squeeze, keeping his unblinking gaze upon the trapped man. "Explain it to me or I will carve every piece of flesh off her body and feed it to you."

"It feels like my skin has been turned inside out and the air is like acid against it. There is also a ringing in my ear. I don't know what other way I can describe it," Brendan sprouted, as the agony continued to intensify.

"It'll do," Darren said, obtaining yet another insight to what it was like to feel what he couldn't.

Darren introduced the tip of the blade to the left side of Brendan's mouth and began to cut, his fighting causing the laceration to become more jagged each passing second.

Brendan's screams were somewhat satisfying to Darren, for he enjoyed the thought of the hurt he was imposing causing so much reactions.

"Stop... please... I'll do anything," Brendan begged, through his disfigured mouth.

His words fell on uncaring ears.

Darren proceeded to place the knife firmly against his belly button. He pushed the blade inward and began to pull it up towards Brendan's chest, causing him to clench his rattling fists and howl towards the ceiling before life slowly left him.

Darren looked down at the two bodies in front of him with a huge smile cutting its way across his face. As the blood dripped from the knife, Darren took a moment to relish his accomplishment, he had experienced pain and the effects of it as close as he ever had in the past.

He realised he couldn't leave the two lumps of meat on display on the shed floor, so he decided to get rid of the bodies and prepare the area for the next occupant that was going to take up residence there. Judging on what he had experienced, Darren wondered was that going to be the closest he would ever get to understanding what pain was and the relationship it had on the body, however he knew there was only one way to find out.

He untied the two bodies and watched them slump over onto the ground, thankful that he had put the bin bags on the floor to entrap the blood and lumps of flesh. Darren quickly wrapped the cold plastic around the bodies and used some of the rope which had held them in position to secure it.

Over the past number of days, he considered numerous locations to hide the remains once he was finished with them, however Darren thought it best to bury them on his property, to help conceal the evidence as best as possible.

He grabbed a shovel, left the shed and walked beyond it to a grouping of trees a short distance away. Choosing a location, Darren stabbed the shovel into the soil and dug a hole large enough to swallow the two corpses, while the reactions of Brendan and Rebecca played over and over in his mind. *Their deaths were worth it,* Darren thought to himself, pushing the shovel into the dirt before collecting the bodies, one at a time.

After unceremoniously rolling the couple into the

ground on top of one another, Darren covered them and double checked the shed to ensure that he didn't leave anything behind. Satisfied he had successfully hidden the evidence, Darren stepped into his kitchen and began to prepare some dinner, all the while looking out in the direction of the freshly dug soil with a smile stretched across his face.

The thought of being caught crossed his mind more than once, however he was sure there was nothing to raise any suspicion towards him. For now, in the public eye, he was a grieving son, who had moved to a different home to try to rebuild his life as much as he possibly could after the tragic loss of his parents.

Chapter 7

The glorious, warm sunlight beat its way down onto Darren's back as he stood over his parent's grave. Deep down inside he knew he would never be able to fill the gaping hole within him, nor forgive himself for causing their deaths.

Stooping down, Darren settled the flowers he had recently placed upon it, which were barely clinging to life due to the recent warm weather. He turned and looked towards the two names etched onto the plate fixed onto the small wooden cross. His parents would be appalled by his recent actions; however he wasn't going to stop.

Returning home, he looked towards the area where he buried the bodies as he parked. Darren needed another subject to continue his self-motivated research, however he knew he couldn't abduct people from the same location because that may raise awareness about him. It had been several days since he tortured the couple on his property and over the previous nights, he decided the Wicklow Mountains would be a good place to seek out his next victim. During the summer months the area attracted quite a number of visitors and hillwalkers, which, if he timed just right, he may be able to overpower one and begin the process all over again.

It was a Saturday evening when Darren decided to drive towards the tourist hotspot. He originally planned to survey the area for a while however, decided that the least amount of time he spent there, the better. He checked his van to ensure he had the equipment necessary to carry out the task and then started the engine.

Darren flicked on the radio and began tapping the steering wheel to the music in the background. Endless possibilities ran through his mind, excitement building within him, he was confident he would come across a late evening jogger as the sun was setting.

Negotiating the narrow, winding roads, Darren was greeted with quite a bit of traffic. As before, this had both a positive and a negative impact on his plans.

Driving through the beautiful area, Darren met groups of people and individuals on their own enjoying the bright evening.

Looking into his rear-view mirror he noticed a car catching up on him, he realised that he had slowed his pace somewhat, trying to decide who the victim was.

He flicked on the indicator and pulled over into a parking area above a deep valley. Darren stepped out of the van, pulled his phone from his pocket and proceeded to take photos of the rock formation glistening in the sun, on the far side, opposite him, in order to give the illusion he was interested in the scenery.

Hearing the car pass him, Darren turned back

towards the road to spot a couple smile to him as they walked past. His attention was then drawn further up the hill he had been driving along. In the distance he eyed a woman on her own, jogging in the late evening sunlight.

"Perfect," Darren said, placing the phone back into his pocket, already running through the numerous ways he would get her to talk.

As he stepped back to his van, Darren's challenge would be to kidnap her without any witnesses. His next thought was that she wouldn't have made her way out to the location on foot. So, it was very likely she parked her vehicle in a parking area further up the road, was carrying out her exercise and would return once finished. A long shot Darren thought, however it was possible, and it would make the task of abducting her somewhat easier if he struck quickly with no one around.

He manoeuvred the van safely back out onto the road and continued up towards her. Passing by, Darren noted she was carrying a water bottle and listening to what he assumed to be music, through her headphones. She had her long blonde hair tied into a pony tail and Darren was sure she was warmer than she would have been if she hadn't worn all black workout clothing.

Darren rounded several more corners to see a group of cars parked in the distance. He reversed his van into the same parking location and waited.

After a few minutes Darren got out of the van and

went for a short walk, while maintaining a good line of sight on the carpark and the road twisting up to it. He decided this approach was better as it would look strange if he just sat in the driver's seat waiting. He once again retrieved his phone and began to randomly take pictures when he saw people come and go from the area.

Looking towards his watch, Darren exhaled deeply noting approximately half an hour had passed and there was still no sign of the woman making her way back towards where he was sure she would have parked. Although there was still a number of cars parked in the area, she may have been picked up Darren thought as he began to make his way back to his van, witnessing another vehicle pull out and make its way down the winding road.

Watching the car disappear, from view, Darren's eyes widened with delight upon seeing the woman running, slower than before, her way back up the steep incline.

Climbing back into his van, Darren knew she was only a few minutes away. He rattled as the anticipation ran through him, monitoring every inch around him to ensure no one was watching.

Two further vehicles moved along the road while he waited, however there was no one in any of the cars around him and from what he could tell, nobody in sight was making their way back from the hills surrounding the area.

Darren's breath ceased momentarily as the woman

slowed to a walking pace and turned left into the car park. His assumption was correct, she had parked there to go for her run.

She made her way to a car situated two spaces away from him as Darren rotated the handle to let down the driver's window.

Checking the area once again, "Sorry, I wonder can you help me?" Darren asked, as she removed her headphones.

The woman didn't react and started stretching behind her car as the sweat on her brow twinkled in the dying sunlight.

"Hello?" Darren called once again.

The woman turned and smiled to him, "Sorry, I didn't realise you were talking to me."

"It's okay, just wondering could you help me with some directions please if you have the time," Darren smiled in response.

"Of course," she replied, and made her way over to him.

"I'm just wondering what is the quickest way back to Dublin from here?" Darren queried, while scanning the area beyond her and quickly glancing into the van mirrors once again.

"Dublin?"

Happy that the road was quiet and no one was present, Darren suddenly grabbed her arm, pulled her towards him and he swiftly wrapped one arm around her throat while placing the other hand on the back of her head. The woman thrashed about for a moment until she was rendered unconscious.

Darren leapt from the van, opened the back door and tossed her inside. Once he bound her hands, he placed duct tape over her mouth.

Stepping back to the driver's door, Darren quickly glanced about the area one final time and was satisfied he had not been seen.

Starting the engine, Darren left the carpark and turned right, greeted seconds later by another car driving up the hill. He smiled, realising he had been just in time, as he politely waved to the unsuspecting people passing by him and drove home.

Flinging open the shed door, Darren stepped inside with his next victim draped over his shoulder. Due to her small frame, it meant he could easily manoeuvre her limp body anyway he desired.

Darren had re-laid the floor with more plastic so he would have minimal cleaning up to do after he was finished with the body. Chaining her to one of the large pillars in the centre room, he made a final check on the shackles before placing a strap tightly around the thick steel and her forehead to hold her head in place as he had done so with Brendan and then turned to his captive.

"Wake up," Darren said, slapping her on the cheek.

"Hey," Darren continued, increasing the strikes against her face.

The woman's eyes slowly opened, instantly noticing the unfamiliar surroundings she began to panic.

"Don't even bother," Darren instructed, grabbing her by her tiny neck. "Whoever you think you can call for help isn't going to hear you. The only thing that matters is this room and the feelings you will experience within it. I want you to project each and every one of them concisely, that's all that matters,"

Her anxiety increased hearing this statement and her gasps for air deepened, which was made difficult by the gag covering her mouth.

"No time like the present I suppose," Darren smiled, not wanting to waste any time.

Before he began, Darren retrieved the woman's phone and placed it onto the bench opposite her. He picked up a hammer and smashed the device into pieces before her terror-filled eyes.

Keeping the hammer in one hand, Darren fetched a nail from the box in front of him and stepped towards his newest victim.

"I just want you to tell me how it feels, okay?" Darren requested before placing the tip of the steel nail into the woman's ear and began tapping it gently inward with the hammer.

Feeling her ear canal expand, the pressure and then the sudden pop, followed by loud ringing, mixed with the worst pain she had ever felt, caused the woman to thrash about on the floor.

Darren stopped and pulled the tape from her mouth.

"Tell me," Darren instructed.

"Help!" The woman screamed as loud as her voice would allow.

Darren placed his grip around her neck once more, "Didn't I just tell you that would do no good? You're wasting my time, tell me how it feels!"

Confusion bugled in her mind, as her eyes raced around the room for a way to escape, however the hard slap to her face drew her attention back to the psychotic man in front of her as the sharp sting continued to vibrate through the side of her head.

Looking deep into the glaring eyes in front of her, the woman concentrated on her breathing to try to help calm the horrible situation she found herself trapped within.

"What do you want? My husband will be looking for me," passed her quivering lips.

"He won't find you, no one will," Darren replied, moving closer to her.

"Please, just let me go. You don't need to do this," the woman said.

"Look. They all say that. They all beg for their lives and offer me alternatives. Do you really think I am going to let you go? You were dead the moment I grabbed you and now you have two choices! You can either tell me how you feel as your body reacts to what it is going through, or, you can just sit there, and I'll take my time while making it hurt so much that all you will be able to do is roar in agony. You decide!" Darren said, standing and returning to the bench of implements he had laid out as the blood continued to trickle from the woman's ear.

"What's your name?" Darren asked, eyes flicking from one possible pain inflicting tool to the next.

The woman scanned the room rapidly as the hopelessness built within her each passing second. Her restraints were wrapped tightly around her wrists, head and neck, the door had been securely closed and locked behind them and there was no indication anyone was close by.

"Name?" The woman heard once again through the ringing dominating her hearing.

"Rachel," she spluttered, noting the window to her left had been crudely covered, and boarded to prevent it being used as a means of escape.

"I need you to be concise for me, it'll be a lot easier," Darren instructed.

Watching him run his hand over the items in front of him, Rachel prayed the door would be kicked open by the Gardaí any moment. A wish that became less realistic as time passed by.

Selecting a vice grip and two cable ties, Darren turned and made his way back to Rachel.

He squatted and wrapped the cable ties around her ankles, listening to her pleas for life as he did so, and pulled them tightly together.

"If you scream needlessly for help, I will smash your teeth and pull what's left of them from your mouth with this," Darren said, holding the cold steel in front of her petrified face. "Don't be confused, you can and will wail, but I don't want you to waste your energy on something that isn't coming."

Darren reached down and untied the laces on her footwear. He pulled them off one at a time and left them to one side.

After he removed the sock from her left foot, Rachel began to squirm about on the plastic laid beneath her.

"Hold still, this won't do you any good," Darren said, as he pulled her legs back into a straight position, then placed his right shin across her knees to help hold her in place.

Darren flicked open the vice grip and adjusted the screw.

When Rachel felt the ice-cold steel jaws surround her baby toe, she again began to beg Darren to stop.

Closing the handle tightly, Rachel felt the pressure of the tool clamping onto her.

"I just want to know," Darren said, turning to her with a blank expression.

Without hesitation, while securing her foot, he quickly pulled the handle back towards Rachel, creating a crunch, causing Rachel to spit in agony. At that moment, the new pain introduced to her body seemed to outweigh the injury caused to her ear.

"Tell me what it is like," Darren commanded.

"What do you want from me, what do you think it feels like?" Rachel cried, eyes unable to focus.

Darren released the snapped toe and tightly grabbed the one next to it. "I hope you explain this one a little better!" Darren said, frustration bubbling within him.

Hearing the next bone shatter and Rachel's cries increase in volume, Darren turned to her once again.

"Well?" his patience about to crack quicker than the toes beneath him.

Inhaling deeply through gritted teeth, Rachel stared back at her captive, "Do it to yourself you sick freak and you'll find out!"

Darren slowly shook his head in disappointment as he realised the toe he had bent in the opposite direction. He quickly placed Rachel's big toe into the vice grip and proceeded to break it, causing the same audible reaction to fill the room as the two previous toes.

"Have it your way," Darren spat, standing upright.

He punched Rachel hard, in anger, and tossed the vice grip aside.

Darren turned and made his way to his kitchen and flicked on the kettle.

Waiting for the water to boil, Darren looked towards the shed which was holding his latest victim captive and wondered would he ever get a true explanation on what he so longed to feel.

Hearing the switch flip off, Darren grabbed the kettle and walked back towards the shed.

Fetching a funnel from the bench, he walked over to Rachel, who, by then was barely holding onto consciousness as the blood pooled beneath her.

"Don't want to talk? Fine, I'll make sure to don't make anymore noise," Darren snarled, loosening the neck and forehead straps so he could tilt her head backward.

Rachel tried her best to fight him off as Darren forced the tip of the funnel into her mouth and continued to push it downward until her gag reflex kicked in.

Watching her struggle for air, Darren raised the kettle full of steaming water and began to pour it into the funnel, causing Rachel's head to rattle about, violently, thumping against the pillar behind her.

The water instantly scalded her lips, tongue and throat and the feeling was unlike anything she had ever experienced before.

During the process, some of the boiling water splashed onto Darren's hand causing absolutely no sensation as he watched his skin turn a bright crimson.

After empting the contents of the kettle, he removed the funnel and Rachel slumped over, whilst heavy, laboured gurgling filled the room as her mouth and throat swelled further each passing second.

"I just wanted you to tell me what it was like, but you can't even do one simple thing," Darren said, storming from the shed, slamming the door behind him.

He went into the house and sat, staring blankly at the wall in front of him. Following the anguish he recently inflicted on people, he had gained very little. Darren was beginning to wonder if he would ever get an answer to satisfy him. He seemed to obtain more from the expressions on their faces and the groans spouting passed their lips than the words they spoke.

I must keep trying. I can't just give up, Darren thought to himself. He knew the more people he kidnapped and eventually killed, the chance of getting caught increased, but he couldn't stop, not now, he had acquired a taste for inflicting torture on his specimens in order to identify how it felt and what he was missing.

Meanwhile Rachel's breathing became more laboured as the night grew thicker.

Regaining consciousness, she felt as though someone had shoved a thick, sharp blade down her throat and was continually spinning the handle. The ringing in her ear was still emitting its tune as she studied the area to see if Darren had left anything nearby following his cruel acts to help her escape, however she couldn't distinguish between the darkness in the room and the objects within it. Each breath caused excruciating pain as she felt her throat close further and further, breaths shortening.

Rachel wished she was back out in the Wicklow Mountains jogging just a few hours previous, she also wished she had ignored Darren when he called her over to him. Her thoughts shot towards her husband, surely, he must be looking for her by now, however what quickly dashed her hopes of rescue was she didn't know where she was and did anyone even see her being dragged into the van and driven away.

Breaths labouring even further, Rachel's panic

increased as she could not by then take large inhales, she felt like she was slowly being strangled internally.

Testing her arm restraints, nothing budged, Rachel tried her leg restraints and yelped as much as her throat would allow when she inadvertently moved her toes, causing the broken ones to emit pain in their protest to moving.

It was no good, she couldn't free herself and even if she did, Rachel wasn't sure how far she would make it due to the condition she was in.

The following morning Darren awoke to beautiful sunshine bouncing off his bedroom window curtains. Spinning on the mattress, he threw his arms out and stretched for a moment, then went to the bathroom to get a shower. After brushing his teeth, Darren stepped into the kitchen and placed two eggs into a saucepan of water.

Waiting for his breakfast to boil, Darren stared through the kitchen window towards the shed housing his latest specimen. Following his meal, Darren would continue his experiments on Rachel.

Stepping out into the sunshine, Darren made his way towards the shed a short distance away.

Glancing around the area, which was surrounded by a heavy treeline and undergrowth, Darren knew it was an ideal location to carry out the acts he was committing, due to it being out of the way and no clear line of sight for some distance.

Reaching the heavy door, he unlocked it and

stepped inside to be greeted with a motionless Rachel in front of him.

"Let us continue, shall we?" Darren said, closing the door behind him.

"You awake?" He asked, turning to her to see she still had not moved position.

As Darren made his way over to his latest captive, he quickly realised she wasn't breathing.

"NO!" Darren spat, racing over to the limp body and shaking it in an effort to revive her. However, it was clear to him by the paleness of her face and lack of breathing that she had been dead quite some time.

"Fuck," Darren exhaled, hanging his head beside her. He had let his frustration get the better of him the day previous and had lost his opportunity to capitalise on having Rachel trapped there.

He undid her restraints and watched the lump of meat fall unto the plastic spread across the floor.

Standing over the body, various thoughts ran through Darren's mind as he tried to come to terms with how he was going to move forward and who would be next to aid him understand life with pain as a component.

Looking at Rachel's body lying face down on the floor, an interesting idea crossed his mind.

Darren turned and retrieved the knife from the bench of implements he had used on his victims over the last number of sessions.

He reached down and sliced open Rachel's t-shirt and bra strap to reveal her bare back. Without any hesitation, Darren began to carve deep into the smooth skin which covered her.

Following some careful cutting, he removed a square piece of flesh from the dead body at his feet.

As he looked at the sliced woman's back, he knew if the same thing was done to him the process would be no more significant than simply cutting his hair.

Turning the flesh in his hand, Darren studied the mixture of bright and dull red with some scattered areas white throughout the meat. He placed the piece of Rachel on the floor beside her, Darren then took a firm hold of her shoulders and rolled the body over onto its back.

Again, Darren picked up the knife, sunk it into her stomach and pulled the skin apart. He knew his and Rachel's flesh looked the exact same underneath, however he just couldn't help himself. Logic said his flesh was the same minus the ability to feel, however his mind continued to attack him with the idea when he could cut someone open, he would be able to pinpoint the exact physical component he was lacking compared to everyone else.

Images of Rachel's torture-ridden face, alongside his previous victims raced to the forefront of his mind. Darren envied Brendan, Rebecca, Rachel and Mary. Before dying, they experienced the most intense sensations of their lives. In his opinion, the only reason their deaths were cruel was due to them not being able to experience it again, multiple times.

Thoughts adjusting, Darren turned his attention

onto what he would do next. Three people were by then missing and very soon the Gardaí would be investigating the disappearances so he would have to ease his research in order to keep the spotlight away from him.

As he did before, Darren wrapped the body in the plastic he laid out on the floor before carrying out the torture.

Digging the grave far deeper and after burying her on top of the other two bodies on his property, Darren decided to disinfect the back of his van with bleach as an added measure, thankful he had only used the back space of it to transport his victims.

Chapter 8

It didn't take long for Johnathan, Rachel's husband, to report her missing to the Gardaí. This was quickly followed by the same Garda station receiving reports that Brendan and Rebecca had not returned home following their summer trip to Arklow.

The initial investigation began with photographs of the three individuals being circulated through every news outlet, however no sightings of the missing individuals were witnessed since the average timeframe of their disappearances was established.

It didn't take long for the investigators to notice the snipped fence leading to Brendan and Rebecca's mobile home, which instantly caused raised suspicion alongside the scuff marks on the flooring in the mobile home. The Gardaí questioned the park manager who informed them that the couple used the mobile home themselves for the most part, however they did from time to time allow other family members and friends to use the facility. This of course would make it very difficult for a forensics examination due to the scattered footfall.

Every inch of the mountainous area where Rachel was snatched was explored by the Gardaí, volunteers and of course her husband. However, the only thing that was discovered was her empty car. Again, due to the amount of people coming and going from the area meant the investigation would be very difficult. So, the next approach the Gardaí decided to take was to talk to individuals who lived close to where the last known whereabouts of the missing people were.

Meanwhile, Darren had spent the last number of days reflecting on what he achieved so far. He had come to the realisation that maybe the closest he would ever get to feeling pain was watching the effects of it on others. He needed more but his head ached trying to decipher a way in which he could gain what he longed for.

Visiting his parent's grave, Darren wondered what they looked like entombed in the cold, dark ground beneath him. How much skin had been eaten away from their bones, he wondered as he leaned down to address the small flower pot which had toppled over due to the wind. Standing once more, the images of their decaying skulls, mouths agape, filled his thoughts. It was then a new idea struck him, after witnessing the terror and more importantly, the pain, etched across his victim's faces, Darren had buried them shortly afterward. All he had was the memories of what they looked like, however if he kept them in a secure location, he would be able to study their last projection of agony in more detail. It may help give him a better understanding, he thought.

Walking back towards his van, Darren considered digging the bodies back up and taking their heads but decided it would be better to start off fresh, and allow the recently disturbed ground on his property settle.

Darren made his way back home, his thoughts flooding with how to target his next victim. He cast his mind back to his school days and how some of the children were afraid of him, while others mocked him for being different.

"We would see who would be laughing if I got my hands on you all now!" Darren said, as he stared off into the distance.

It was when he caught sight of home that Darren eyed the squad car parked at the entrance to his property. Darren gripped the steering wheel tighter, his mind racing, wondering if he had over looked something. Nothing obvious jumped out as he pulled the van to a halt beside the Gardaí.

"Darren?" The male Garda asked, stepping out of the car, followed by the female Garda.

"Yes, how can I help you?" Darren smiled, in the friendliest way he could, even though he wished them dead in his mind.

"I am Garda Byrne, this is Garda Cullen," he said gesturing to his partner. "We have a number of questions for you."

"Okay, am I in some kind of trouble?" Darren returned, already gauging the best way to attack and overcome them.

"No, we just want to speak to you in relation to some missing people," Garda Cullen responded.

"No problem. Do you want to follow me up to the

house?" Darren asked, opening the large gate in front of the two vehicles, fully aware of who he was going to be quizzed about.

The Gardaí agreed as Darren drove ahead, stopped, stepped out and closed the behind the Garda car so no one else could freely drive in behind them.

Continuing towards his house, Darren parked his van in front of the grave holding the butchered, decaying corpses on his property, in order to conceal it.

"Can I get you anything?" Darren asked, as they followed him to the sitting room.

"No thanks, we are investigating the disappearance of a couple from the holiday park. Have you seen either one of these individuals?" Garda Byrne asked, showing Darren a photograph of the couple he had brutally tortured, while his partner took out a small notebook and pen to jot down Darren's reply. "Have you noticed any suspicious activity over the last number of days?" Garda Cullen added.

Darren took the picture in his hand and stared a moment at the glowing smiles in front of him, happiness he recently erased from the world and buried just a short distance away.

"Unfortunately, I can't say that I have," Darren said, hands steady and no hint of uneasiness in his tone. "Do you know what happened?"

"We can't go into too much detail I'm afraid, however we are still in the early stages of the investigation," Garda Cullen outlined.

"It's a busy area isn't it?" Darren added handing the photograph back to the Gardaí. "I see a lot of unfamiliar people around here due to the holiday park, so it's hard to keep track if that makes sense?"

"I understand. So, nothing out of the ordinary?"

"Nothing I can think of anyway. I like keeping to myself. It's usually into town and back, that's about as far as I go," Darren returned, picturing the blonde, uniformed woman, standing in front of him screaming for her life as he slowly cut into her flesh.

"Have you ever been to the park?"

"No, I wouldn't know even one person in there. Like I said, I just keep to myself. I enjoy my own company."

"You have quite a large piece of land here. Have you had any trouble with trespassing?" Garda Byrne continued.

"Not that I am aware of. No one bothers me here and that's how I like it," Darren smiled.

"We have another missing person. Have you seen this woman?" Darren was quizzed, as he was handed a picture of Rachel.

Again, Darren took time to examine the image in front of him, while remembering her pleas in agony as he savoured the reactions. He visualised her torment so much he almost forgot the Gardaí were in the room with him.

"No, again I'm sorry, I'm afraid I haven't seen her either," Darren lied, moments later. "Is she from the area?"

"As I said, we can't give away too much information at the moment. We are trying to gather it for now," was the response from Garda Byrne.

"Okay, well you are more than welcome to look around the property if you wish," Darren replied, hoping his openness would steer their curiosity away from him.

A solution which repeated over and over in Darren's thoughts was beating the pair unconscious, subjecting them to the same process he had carried out on his previous victims and driving the car into the sea not far from his house. However, it was too risky. Chances were that, unprepared, they may get away and reinforcements would be called within minutes. No. Darren decided he would have to maintain a cool nerve.

"Thank you. We may need to at some stage, for now our only concern is gathering information to help us establish the last movements of the missing parties," Garda Cullen said, closing the notepad and placing it back into her pocket.

"I understand," Darren replied. "Well if I think of, or hear anything I'll be the first one to let know you," he continued, smiling to the Gardaí in front of him.

"We appreciate it. You may see us around a lot more until we get to the bottom of this, so it'll be easy to get in touch, however, here is my contact details just in case," Garda Byrne said, handing Darren his card.

"Of course," Darren returned before leading the individuals from his home.

Watching the car disappear down the drive, Darren clenched his fists harder with each passing second. He wondered if he had overlooked something which in turn led the Gardaí to his doorstep but rationalised he would be currently in the back of their car if he had done so.

Closing the door, Darren stepped into the sitting room and sat down. He foresaw the Gardaí getting involved at some stage due to his activities, however not as soon. Darren was in a difficult position, should he continue on his current path and risk being caught, or step back for some time and allow the investigations to go cold.

However, his obsession would not allow him to stop. His only purpose was to inflict as much pain as possible in order to decipher its effects on the person he was doing it to.

Chapter 9

Several days had passed since the investigation began into the disappearances.

During this period, Darren spent much of his time within the confines of his home working through several thoughts crashing around his mind. Gaining very little sleep, Darren's conclusion was that his main goal was to carry on working towards narrowing the distance between him and his understanding of pain with the human body.

Darren also considered the involvement of the Gardaí. He wasn't going to let them get in the way of his objective. His obsession had consumed him, even if it meant death, he needed to keep going.

But who would be next? Darren questioned himself, sitting in the comfortable chair, daydreaming out through the window. In his opinion it could be literally anyone he chooses because no one on this Earth could hurt him and if he did get caught by the Gardaí, he could just slit his own throat while laughing in their faces. It was better to do that than spend years in prison, plus the only thing he was living for now was inflicting hurt on others. If he was robbed of that ability, there would be no more need for him to stay alive.

A satisfying idea then crossed Darren's mind. He

cast his thoughts back to his school days, which was accompanied by the bullying he had endured for some time.

"They wouldn't laugh now!" Darren reminded himself, grinning, visualising the countless ways he would enjoy turning their mocking into pleas for help.

It was beneficial that the most recent victims didn't know Darren, he felt it allowed their true emotions to surface. However, he wanted to try his experiments with someone who knew him to see if it would yield different results. One name which presented itself more than once during his reflection was Derek.

Derek O' Brien was one of the main perpetrators of his torment in his school days and was the only individual Darren was sure still lived in the locality, with his girlfriend.

On occasion they bumped into one another since adulthood and each time Derek would cast a smile towards Darren, however it was a smile which Darren couldn't decide if it was genuine or another form of mockery.

Selecting Derek had its positives, he, like Darren, lived in the countryside just outside Arklow, on the opposite side of town, which would make it somewhat easier to get him back to Darren's property.

The excitement began to sprint through Darren's veins visualising the many methods of torture he would soon impose and if Derek's girlfriend got in the way, then so be it.

Darren decided it would be better to establish the pair's routines sooner rather than later in order to develop their pattern and an opportunity to strike as swiftly as possible.

Reaching down, Darren picked up the sharp steak knife which had sat beside him for more hours than he could recall. He placed the edge of the blade against his right forearm.

Pressing downward, Darren pulled the blade back towards him and observed his flesh slice open as the blood began to pour from it with no sensation. At that moment he wished he was inflicting the injury upon Derek, at least then it would have some physical meaning. Darren had seen quite a lot of blood recently, each person's bodily fluid looking exactly like his. Again, he cast his mind to what exactly was missing from him.

A thought suddenly jumped forward. One which he had not contemplated before.

"If I consumed a piece of them while they were experiencing what I was doing to them, maybe it would give me a better understanding," Darren said, beneath his breath, starring at the vital fluid continuing to flow from his arm.

The rational part of him knew it was impossible, however the obsessive portion, the element which now fuelled him, laid the seed in his mind at the small possibility. The secret had to be in there somewhere, he thought, looking down once more at the fresh wound on his body.

Standing, Darren went into the kitchen and bandaged his arm tightly. It was something he needed to be very sure of, because he didn't want the wound bursting open when he invaded Derek's house, leaving any evidence behind him.

Glancing towards the unmarked grave on his property, a grin etched its way across Darren's face. The power and the control were addictive, even though he still hadn't achieved what he set out to do, the terror in his victim's eyes and the agony projected from their expressions was somewhat satisfying.

As nightfall descended, Darren climbed into his van and made his way into Arklow. Passing by the ruins of a burnt down house, where he had killed Mary, Darren's confidence grew. So far, the Gardaí were none the wiser to his activities and if he continued to carry out effective planning, he would remain one step ahead.

Driving through the busy town, Darren took in the sight of many people enjoying themselves at the local pubs. His attention shot to the amber, then solid red light before him. A small group of intoxicated people stumbled across the road in front of him, waving and mocking the vehicle as they did.

"Keep it up, I'll rip it off and feed it to your girlfriend beside you!" Darren grunted, staring towards one of the young men pointing towards him laughing. He didn't remove his icy, unblinking gaze from the individual, now at the back of the group, whose laughter had become a concerned expression due to the intensity of Darren's stare towards him.

The flashing glimmer projected from the amber light pulled Darren's attention back to the road. Darren smirked, visualising what he could do to him, and continued to make his way towards Derek's home.

With the town lights now a distant glow against the clear night sky, Darren navigated the winding uphill road towards his next victim's house.

Locating a vacant gateway near his destination, Darren pulled the van over and switched off the engine. As before, he wanted to establish exactly how many people he would be dealing with when it came the time to strike.

Reaching the entrance to Derek's home, Darren eyed the dancing television light ricocheting against the walls in what he assumed to be the sitting room. His mind returned to the images and little information gained from his previous victims, clenching his fists, Darren hoped that Derek and his girlfriend, if she was in the house with him, would perform much better.

Reaching down, Darren slowly unlatched the gate to the home and made his way towards the fully exposed window. Darren considered removing his footwear as he did before in order to cover himself, however he was walking on a hard surface and wasn't planning on entering the house before carrying out further information gathering on the area and the people who dwelled there.

Peering in over the window sill, Darren noticed the top of the window was ajar as he spotted Derek sitting on a large, comfortable looking sofa, with his arm wrapped around his girlfriend. Her name escaped Darren, however he didn't care, if she lived there, she was on the list too.

Without warning, the Jack Russell Terrier resting beside the couple, raised its head and began to growl which trigged Darren to quickly drop below the window.

"What's wrong with you?" Derek's girlfriend smiled, as the small dog climbed up and moved across the couple's laps.

"Probably a cat or something," Derek laughed.

Meanwhile, Darren hoped he wasn't seen as he hadn't prepared nor aimed to take the pair during his first visit to the property.

The dog continued to snarl, which caused Derek's amusement to turn to suspicion.

"I'll go check it out," Derek said, lifting himself to his feet.

"Do you want me to pause the show for you?" The beautiful blonde haired, blue-eyed woman asked.

"No, no, I'll be two seconds."

Derek made his way to the front door, flicking on the hallway and outside lights.

Opening the door, the Jack Russell sprinted passed Derek and quickly disappeared into the darkness in front of him.

"Ben," Derek called, once he lost sight of him, his barking increasing.

Thankfully, the perimeter of the site was fully fenced which meant he couldn't get out.

"Is everything okay?" A voice called from behind Derek.

Turning, Derek's mouth widened and his blood ran cold, seeing a dark figure looming behind his girlfriend.

"Susan!" Derek roared.

She only had a split second to process the terror on Derek's face before she received a devastating blow to the back of her head from Darren's fist.

"You should always lock your doors," Darren grinned to Derek.

Without a second thought, Derek sprinted towards Darren and the pair fell to the ground. Fighting for position, Derek delivered three rapid punches to Darren's face which instantly caused swelling to begin, however this was the only effect it had on him as he began to laugh at the pointless attempts to cause him discomfort.

Allowing further punches to connect, Darren finally reached up, forced his right thumb into Derek's eye, hooked the socket and pulled his head to one side, accompanied by a left fist of his own, causing Derek to fall hard to the ground beside him.

Eye blinded and pain running through him, Derek tried to distribute further punches to Darren, however they had no impact.

"Absolutely pathetic," Darren growled, before he drew back and kicked Derek in the stomach.

"What do you want?" Derek asked, when the air finally returned to his lungs to fuel the words, still unaware who exactly had attacked him and his girlfriend.

"You know I didn't want it to happen so quickly. I wanted to gather some information before I took you both, but that stupid animal just wouldn't shut up." Darren replied, sitting down on the chair beside Susan who was still face down on the floor.

"Darren," Derek groaned, finally looking up and realising who the attacker was. "What are you doing? Stop now before you do something you'll regret!"

"Regret? The only regret I have is that I can't feel what is making you grimace so much right now," Darren snapped back, leaning forward, hands clasped with his elbows on his knees.

Hearing the response, Derek tried to lift himself from the carpet beneath him.

"Don't even bother," Darren instructed, setting a well-placed foot on the back of Susan's head.

"Please, don't do this," pleas similar to the ones Darren had heard quite a lot recently.

"Remember when you used to make fun of me for being different?" Darren quizzed, eyes still locked on the man opposite him. "Remember pointing at me and laughing, encouraging everyone else to do the same!"

"Jesus Darren, we were only children, is that what this is about?" Derek replied, a trickle of blood now passing his lips.

"No, it goes far beyond that, you will make a nice project."

Derek, confusion carved across his face, lay on the floor looking towards Darren and his helpless girlfriend contemplating the various possibilities of overpowering Darren and seeking help.

Without warning, Ben began to bark frantically outside the front door.

"Shut that mutt up now and if you try anything, I'll crush her neck!" Darren said, pressing down harder on Susan.

Derek, body aching, slowly raised himself to his feet. Disorientation quickly befell him due to the vicious eye injury as he began to stumble his way to the door.

"Hold on a second, where are your phones?"

"What?" Derek asked, turning back towards him.

"Your mobile phones, how stupid do you think I am? I'm not letting you out of this room so you can call for help. Before you go anywhere put the phones on the table," Darren instructed, pointing towards the small piece of furniture in the centre of the room.

Witnessing the intensity in Darren's eyes, Derek reached into his pocket, pulled out his phone and placed it flat on the table as Ben's barking grew louder and louder.

"Hers?" Darren asked, Derek standing motionless,

knowing the situation was becoming worse.

"HER PHONE?"

"It's in her left front pocket," Derek replied.

Darren reached down and quickly snatched the phone, eyes remaining firmly fixed on Derek. "Okay go shut that dog up or I will," he instructed.

Derek stepped into the small hallway beside the sitting room and opened the front door. Ben tried his best to race past him, however Derek quickly snatched the tiny animal in his arms and locked him into the spare room to his right.

Meanwhile Darren, leaving Susan on the floor, quickly went to the kitchen and fetched the first razor sharp knife he could find. He returned to the sitting room, took hold of Susan's hair in his fists and dragged her upward onto his knee. He grabbed the knife once again in his right hand and began to thump the base of the handle against her temple to help her regain consciousness.

Susan began to come to her senses as her boyfriend stepped back into the room. His heart sank even further watching Darren hold the blade to her throat.

"Have you got any rope or cable ties?" Darren asked, pressing the blade hard against Susan's soft, bare skin.

"What?" Derek returned.

"Don't keep questioning me, you're starting to annoy me already, if you continue to do so I'm going to slice pieces off her and toss them over to you, understand?" Darren snapped. "Now. Cable ties or rope?"

The threat fuelling his response, Derek replied with "Yes, I think I have some out in the shed."

"Well, let's go," Darren smiled, standing to his feet, lifting Susan with him. "If either one of you try anything, I'll slash this tiny neck open!" he warned, following Derek through the kitchen.

Stepping out into the night air, Derek's instinct was to race into the darkness in search of help, however his flight response was paralysed by the risk posed to his beloved girlfriend, he couldn't live with himself if he just left her there in the grips of a lunatic.

Derek unlatched the door to the shed, flicked on the light and instantly spotted many items he could use to beat his captor with, however he knew the possibility of losing Susan in the process was too great.

"Here they are," Derek said, collecting the plastic bag filled with thick cable ties.

"Okay they'll do. Back inside," Darren said, standing aside to allow Derek to pass.

Once back within the small kitchen, Darren instructed Susan to securely wrap one of the cable ties around Derek's wrists.

Hearing the piece of plastic banding click tightly, Darren reached forward, took hold of the cable tie and pulled as hard as he could on the waste piece, causing Derek to wince and a deep indent on his skin.

"Okay now his ankles," Darren instructed.

Tears saturating her face, Susan did as ordered, feeling the sharp, cold steel pressing firmly against her flesh.

Again, Darren reached for the tie, pulled it tighter and shoved Derek, causing him to fall to the floor with a heavy thud.

"Sit down," Darren ordered Susan, causing her to unleash loud, desperate cries of despair.

"Stop wasting your energy on something non-productive. Now put your wrists together," Darren continued, with the knife in one hand, a thick cable tie in the other.

Susan looked towards her helpless boyfriend on the floor beside her, desperation in his eyes, then she turned her attention back Darren. "Please, you don't have to do this, we can forget the whole thing, we won't say a word to anyone," she pleaded.

No further words passed Darren's lips as he placed the blade onto the table and quickly secured her hands tightly together with no obstruction.

Susan looked to Derek once again, her body unceremoniously being shoved around as her legs were bound together. It was at that very moment Derek couldn't establish what was worse, the inability to help Susan or the look of anguish on her face.

"Everything is going to be okay," Derek sprouted.

"No, it won't!" Darren barked.

Grabbing a handful of her hair once more, Darren lifted Susan from the chair and tossed her to the floor on the opposite side of the room.

He grabbed the tea towel from the counter and rummaged through the drawer beneath the sink, finally finding a pair of scissors. Darren cut the towel in two and stooped over Derek,

"Have you any bleach here?"

"Under the sink," Derek groaned.

Without warning Darren shoved the piece of cloth into Derek's mouth as far as possible, connected two cable ties in order to achieve enough length, then raised Derek's head and bound the cloth in place, as Derek's eyes painfully widened as the end was pulled tight.

Darren carried out the same process with Susan before he closed the back door firmly behind him and cautiously made his way back towards his parked vehicle.

The night had not unfolded exactly how he anticipated but Darren needed to adapt to the situation, while remaining as anonymous as he possibly could. Pacing in the direction of his van, senses heighted, a tug of war was occurring in Darren's mind, due to the endless possibilities of torture he was going to inflict on the couple.

Thankful no traffic had passed him, Darren started the engine, drove the short distance and parked in front of Derek and Susan's home. He opened the gate to their driveway and reversed the van as close as he possibly could to the front door.

With the bright moonlight caressing his back,

Darren re-entered the house to find the couple had wriggled closer to one another, however the distance between them still too great to begin any form of escape.

"I admire the fight in you both," Darren stated, picking Susan up onto his shoulder. "I hope you can use that energy in more positive ways when we get back to my place."

After securing Susan, Darren returned to the kitchen, grabbed Derek and dragged him towards the open doors on his van. Derek moaned as his body weight came into contact with the saddle boards in the doorways, however it was nothing compared to what he was going to experience.

Satisfied the pair were locked into the back of the van, Darren returned to the kitchen, fetched the bleach from beneath the sink and the brush from the hallway.

Starting with the back door handle, he made his way through the house, bleaching everything he had come into contact with, switching off each room light as he did so. Darren also scrubbed the floor and finished by bleaching the front door handle. He repeated the process at the gate to their house after closing it behind him, then he departed for home.

Chapter 10

The following morning Darren drove into town once he double checked his two captives were firmly tied to the large, steel pillars in the centre of the shed, the very same location where he had inflicted so much suffering on his previous prisoners.

During his journey through Arklow, Darren consumed the happiness of the locals around him while they enjoyed the beautiful, warm sunshine and each other's company. He of course could witness beauty; however he could not feel it, something as simple as appreciating the warmth of a summer's day was alien to him.

However, the concern still remained within him. *What if I have gotten as close as I ever will?* Darren thought in relation to truly knowing what pain felt like on the body, what anything physically felt like for that matter.

He parked at the local hardware shop and stepped inside, instantly taking note of the newspaper tucked beneath the arm of one shopper, the headline still looking for information on the disappearances of Brendan, Rebecca, and Rachel. A smirk crossed Darren's face remembering their cries and expressions of agony, however he needed to experience more. Yes, the power and control were extremely satisfying to him, but the main goal was to encounter as much as he could to help build his understanding.

Moving through the shop, Darren stopped at an area which displayed woodworking chisels both in sets and others sold individually. He moved further through the aisles, Darren had used knives, vice grips, a screwdriver and so on to initiate pain, however he was looking for something different to add to the equation.

Rounding a corner, Darren spotted the power tool section, which conveniently had a promotional sale running. His eyes widened with intrigue taking in the vast array of implements which included saws, drills and sanders, however his attention rested on a small, battery operated angle grinder sitting to his right.

Perfect! Darren thought, picking it up off the shelf. He had seen them used in the past during his working days and rationalised that the added noise from the piece of equipment would induce a higher rate of fear, which in turn may cause the victim to open up more.

Darren engaged in worthless small talk at the checkout counter and returned home, instantly placing the battery of the grinder on charge.

While waiting, Darren stepped out towards the shed in his back yard. He paused for a moment at the door and listened to the low murmuring come from the gagged couple inside. Out of nowhere, a thought of his parents jumped into his mind as it had done so many times recently, causing Darren to lower his hand from the lock. He daydreamed a moment, knowing they would be angry at the terrible acts he had carried out, however he needed to move forward- he had to feed his obsession.

Brushing the images of his parents aside, Darren slotted the key into the lock and stepped inside, greeted with worried looks projected towards him from Derek and Susan as he opened the door. Excitement erupted within him once more, witnessing their desperation and sheer hopelessness.

"This will be the most important day of your lives," Darren stated, flicking on the light switch and closing the door behind him. "You will help me understand something you have, which I never will. All I need you both to do is explain everything in detail when we start."

He walked over to the petrified couple, Derek's wrists now bleeding due to the tightness of the cable ties holding them together. Judging by the depth of the cuts, Darren was sure he tried to break free from them more than once.

"Don't beg, don't offer me anything, don't try to escape and most of all don't think this is about you!" Darren explained.

On the work bench over Darren's shoulder still sat the bloodied items he used on the previous people he experimented on. He considered cleaning them after each use, just in case his property was searched, but decided if it ever came to that stage, the Gardaí would have gathered some evidence on him to do so in the first place.

Darren turned and retrieved a pair pliers from the bench. "If either one of you shout for help, I'll kill the other in front of you. If you don't follow my instructions, I'll rip your throat out as your lover waits to be next. Nod if you understand!"

Both Derek and Susan slowly did so in response.

Grinning towards Derek, Darren raised the pliers and snapped the cable tie away from Susan's face. This was followed by removing the tea towel from her mouth.

Susan's jaw ached while she observed Darren raise the pliers once more and grip her upper lip tightly.

Squeezing on the handle further, Darren pulled slowly downward as Susan's eyes began to swell.

"Remember what I said!" Darren reminded her as he continued to pull her lip further down her face.

Susan wanted to thrash about and scream for help, however her love for Derek would not allow her to do so.

"How does it feel?" Darren quizzed, releasing his tight hold on the pliers.

"Cold. I can feel the force of the jaws on the pliers squeezing my skin to a point where I thought it was about to burst, there was a lot of pressure and I was sure my skin was going to tear when you pulled down on it. I can taste the steel on my tongue," Susan explained, eyes fixed firmly on her boyfriend securely bound beside her.

Darren closed his eyes momentarily and analysed her words, "Very good, how do you think it would feel if I did rip your lips from your face?"

Susan couldn't help but allow the panic to rattle through her, "I'm not sure, but it would be the most painful thing I have ever experienced."

"I agree," Darren replied, glancing to Derek.

Suddenly Darren clamped her upper lip once again with the pliers and with one forceful tug, he ripped a chuck of flesh from her smooth, beautiful face. Without hesitation, Darren tossed the piece of meat into his mouth and began chewing. Darren then placed his hand upon her forehead and pushed her head back to keep her face upright as Susan squealed in agony.

"Concentrate, tell me what you are feeling. What is causing you to react like this?" Darren queried, hoping while ingesting a piece of Susan, accompanied with her descriptions, would help him achieve his goal. Derek was horrified by what he was witnessing.

"It feels like my mouth is on fire, and the pain is spreading across my face," Susan slurred, the warm blood smothering her words.

"And?" Darren quizzed further, the words quickly becoming non-satisfying, as too was his tiny meal.

"And I want it to stop," Susan spat, her face swelling, her tears added to the pain once they reached the exposed flesh.

"I'm afraid that's not going to happen," Darren confirmed, gulping down the piece of Susan.

Following those words Darren reached forward with the pliers once again, this time gripping a chunk of skin on her cheek. Clamping tightly, he placed his left palm on Susan's forehead and began to slowly pull with his right hand, causing her to scream as the flesh began to stretch away from the bone underneath.

"Tell me," Darren demanded, waiting for the meat to digest within him and reveal some kind of result.

The only response was agonising cries, as Derek thrashed about on the floor, helplessly trying to prevent any further harm being inflicted on Susan.

"You were doing so well!" Darren growled, releasing the pliers, examining the deep, dark indents left on her cheek.

"I hope you do better than this," Darren said, staring, intensely through Derek.

Darren tossed the implement he used to deface Susan onto the bench as he walked past it, unlatched the shed door and made his way towards his house.

Looking towards the angle grinder battery charger, Darren witnessed that the tiny light was still a glowing red, indicating the battery still had not reached full charge. However, he was confident it would have enough life in it to do what he needed it to.

Darren clicked the battery into place on the tool and made his way back to Derek and Susan.

"I'm going to try something a little different with you," Darren said, closing the door firmly behind him again, grabbing the sharp knife from the bench and made his way over to Derek.

A massive grin spread across Darren's face looking at the defenceless man in front of him. Darren sat the grinder on the floor and reached down and took hold of Derek's bound ankles, then kneeled across his thighs. From previous experience, Darren established it was a very good way to control a person's movements. Taking hold of Derek's pants, Darren used the knife to slice upward through the cloth on the left leg, stopping just above the knee. He pulled the material to one side and cut it away completely. Darren grasped the power tool and flicked it to life, the noise bombarding Susan and Derek's ears.

"Hold very, very still," Darren instructed, as he took hold of the cable tie around Derek's head.

With precise actions, he pulled the thick piece of plastic away from Derek's face as much as possible and glanced the rotating disc against it causing it to snap and the cloth used to gag him to fall from his mouth.

"Don't," Derek pleaded, watching Darren lower the edge of the disc towards his shin.

"What do you feel right now?" Darren asked, speaking loudly, so his voice could be heard.

Derek didn't respond as he waited for the tool to rip into his flesh.

Staring at the disc spinning just millimetres from Derek's leg, Darren held his ankles firmly to the floor and slowly grazed the skin causing Derek to howl out as the flesh shredded apart.

"What do you feel?"

No description would be good enough, Darren wanted to study the reaction of the body and the expressions it caused on his victims.

He stared at Derek's mouth agape, eyes shooting to the roof of the shed.

Derek raced for a possible solution which may help him and Susan escape their sadistic entrapment however, his thoughts kept snapping back to the intense burning sensation making its way up along his shin. His teeth reached snapping point as Derek's jaws clamped together when Darren reintroduced the power tool to his prisoner's torn flesh.

"Sore? Explain it!" Darren asked, as he ran the rotating disc up toward the knee.

Derek could only use the gasps of air in his lungs to roar louder and louder feeling his skin being cut away from him.

"Pitiful!" Darren snarled.

With that statement, Darren positioned the edge of the angle grinder above Derek's knee and waited a moment. "Neither of you will be able to help me will you?"

Without an ounce of hesitation, Darren forced the disc down into Derek's knee, causing him to pass out seconds later.

Susan watched in despair, listening to the crunches and the angle grinder noise levels vary due to the pressure applied during her boyfriend's limb removal. A sickly taste bubbled on her tongue witnessing

Darren bend the leg to one side, causing the wound to open further so he could continue the cut, while the blood flowed around the plastic beneath them.

Darren studied the meat and knee joint separate with intrigue. He thought it a pity the immense agony caused Derek to lose consciousness, however there was no stopping Darren now.

"Isn't it amazing what holds us together?" Darren said, flicking off the switch, holding the severed limb in front of Susan.

Her tears clouded her vision, as her boyfriend's blood dripped onto her thighs.

"I mean when everything is considered, we aren't very durable at all are we? A simple paper cut can cause bleeding; however I have never known what that feels like and I finally realise now that I never will. Pain is something I will never experience, but it is something I can create!"

Susan turned her head in the opposite direction as far as she possibly could before Darren grabbed her chin and forced her face back to him.

"Please stop this," Susan said, eyes firmly closed.

"Open them or I'll cut off your eyelids. You'll see this freely or by force," Darren replied.

Susan knew it would mean nothing to him to snip away the tiny pieces of skin covering her eyes.

Watching his conscious victim do as she was instructed, Darren continued. "If I did the exact same thing to your leg, it would look the same, if I cut off mine just like his, it would look the same. But there is something missing from me, something you can't see," Darren said, before pulling a piece of ravaged skin from the limb and tossing it onto his taste deprived tongue.

As vomit gurgled in her throat, Susan could sense the disappointment in Darren's tone as he stood upright and flung Derek's leg to the floor beside him.

Darren stepped over to the workbench and took hold of the knife he previously used on his targets. He turned, walked back to Derek, and kneeled on one knee beside him.

"If you look away, I'll slice open his throat," Darren confirmed. "The face can portray so many different feelings, I would love to know how he felt as he passed out. Time to preserve that expression," Darren continued, digging the tip of the blade into Derek's face.

Susan watched in terror as her captor pulled the knife in a circular motion, revealing a crimson, thin line in the skin behind it.

"Derek, please wake up," Susan pleaded.

Wasting no time, Darren pinched a piece of the sliced skin on Derek's forehead, inserted the blade behind it, and slowly started to skin him.

Minutes later, Darren had Derek's face in his hands while Susan cursed him for carrying out such a sadistic act on the love of her life.

Darren's first response was a smile and he placed the skin onto the bench behind him.

"No point in dragging it out I suppose," Darren

said, before plunging the knife into Derek's stomach rapidly several times.

"You bastard! You'll rot in prison for this," Susan spat as best she could past her deformed mouth.

"It's really not a good time to be making threats," Darren replied, turning to her. "Let's see what expression makes its way across your beautiful face now shall we."

Darren dropped the knife to his feet and lunged on top of the helpless woman, wrapping his hands firmly around her throat.

Susan's eyes bulged wildly as she gagged for oxygen.

"That's it, show me... show me more of your pain," Darren commanded, squeezing tighter and tighter.

She shock about violently as her lungs battled to expand with air.

"Your final expression will be mine forever."

Susan grimaced, eyes fixed on him, before she finally became limp in Darren's hands.

Darren retrieved the knife, while watching his victim's head slump to one side. He carried out the same process with precision in order to remove her face from the muscle and nerves beneath it.

Even though the flesh had no structure or firmness behind it, Darren was satisfied he captured both Derek and Susan's final, painful expressions within the tissue.

Darren sat Susan's face beside her boyfriend's on

the bench opposite the mutilated and disfigured bodies. He stared a moment at the eyeless pieces of meat, amazed at the reaction he achieved due to the various torture methods he inflicted on the pair.

Darren knew for sure no matter how much people explained themselves, no words would ever be good enough for him and judging by his current state, ingesting his victims yielded no results either. However, the power and control he witnessed while carrying out his heinous acts was addictive and he knew there was no way he was going to stop.

Suddenly another interesting thought crossed his mind. He was going to keep the faces of his victims as trophies, however Darren wanted to observe the agony he caused and for it to be available to him at any time he wished, so he unlatched the shed door and stepped inside his house.

Darren rummaged through the drawers in his bedside locker and fetched a needle and thread.

He promptly returned to the shed and removed his t-shirt to reveal his long, slender frame. Darren then carefully threaded the needle, being sure to double up on the thread for extra strength.

Selecting Derek's face first, he placed the dead man's skin against the centre of his chest. Witnessing a small trickle of blood flow down towards his belly button, Darren wasted no time pushing the needle through Derek's flesh and into his own. As expected, there was no sensation while he worked his way around the edge of the carved face. Once it was secured in place, Darren picked up Susan's face, placed it beneath Derek's and stitched it firmly into position.

Infection was a possibility; however Darren was confident that if he kept the stitches and skin clean it would help prevent it, plus it would mean nothing to him if the wounds became septic.

Darren stood a moment looking down at the faces which were now a part of him. He ran his right hand over them, in a way their pain was now his and this was the closest satisfaction Darren would ever get.

He pulled his t-shirt back on, taking note of the tiny creases the faces beneath it caused and began to clean up the scene.

Firstly, Darren wrapped the bodies in the plastic he had laid on the floor as he had done previously. Once secure, he went to the shallow grave where the decomposing bodies of Brendan, Rebecca, and Rachel lay. Darren considered tying them upright in the shed as ornaments, however it would be too risky and they would surely draw a lot of rodents to the area.

Digging through the loose soil, it did not take Darren long to reach the corpses as the pungent stench bombarded the air around him.

Usually the smell of a rotting cadaver would induce a vomiting reaction, however not with Darren, he couldn't sense it whatsoever. When he removed the earth covering the dark bin bags, he wished he was able to gain more from them.

Ensuring the hole was big enough to swallow the two extra bodies, Darren covered them and retired to his home for the evening.

Flicking on the television, Darren lowered himself onto the soft chair opposite the screen. Not wasting any time, Darren raised his t-shirt and looked down towards the faces sewn to his chest. He noticed more blood had run down his torso and dried into him, however that was not what he concentrated on. Darren rested his arms on the armrests on either side of him and stared at Derek and Susan's mouths. He could still hear the screams they produced due to his actions. Those cries would always be with him, he would never forget them, and their skin was embedded with their final, painful, moments of life, the closest he would ever get to it himself.

Chapter 11

Darren spent the next number of days at home reflecting on what he accomplished and on the limitations of his objective. Eating pieces of his victims hadn't worked but at least he could still examine their faces. The bruising from the altercation with Derek had eased greatly, however, Darren knew eventually the Gardaí would come knocking on his door again because there was only so many people who can go missing before a trend is established. The question which ran through Darren's mind was what would he do when they did visit his property again?

Food supplies were running low, so he needed to go to town, however Darren decided to stop by his parent's grave before visiting the supermarket.

Although he had no sense of smell, the people who he was going to bump into along the way would probably notice something was off due to the two pieces of dead flesh attached to his body. So, with this in mind, Darren sprayed himself with deodorant and then put a coat on to conceal the faces on his chest.

It was a beautiful Saturday afternoon and when Darren stepped out into the bright sunshine, he wished he could feel the warm hugs as it washed over him. He made his way to his van, the vehicle which had helped him so much in recent times, switched on the engine and drove in towards the local cemetery.

"Hello," Darren said, greeting others visiting their loved ones resting place as he passed by them.

Moving through the field of headstones, Darren thought of the many screams which were emitted by the people lying below his feet before they were enclosed there forever. He also thought of the emotional pain shared by the family as they lowered the coffin into the ground.

The flesh on the most of the bodies beneath his feet would have been eaten or rotted away and laying one person beside another, it would be difficult to establish who was who at first sight. This was one of the reasons Darren decided to begin harvesting his victim's faces, their expressions of suffering he imposed on them would be embedded and evident to him for quite some time.

"Hi Darren, how have you been?" A voice called from behind him.

Turning, Darren eyed an elderly man limbering his way up the path towards him, using a walking stick to help him along his way. His name was James, a friend of Darren's deceased father, who was visiting his wife's resting place.

"I'm not too bad thanks, how are you? It's been a while," Darren replied, already examining him, thoughts of punishment racing to the forefront.

"It looks like we all have the same idea today, eh?" James smiled, leaning slightly forward, two withering, freckled hands resting on the walking stick.

"Yeah I guess so. I still can't believe they are gone. I visit as much as I can," Darren replied, the general chit chat meaning absolutely nothing to him.

Eyes monitoring the old, slender frame in front of him, Darren visualised kicking the stick out from under him and watching his feeble body crash to the ground. He would then stamp hard onto one of his limbs, hopefully snapping it, and analyse the reaction it caused, however the pair were in a public place, with people nearby.

"Me too. Makes you wonder doesn't it?" James replied, unaware of the danger he was just a few paces from.

"What's that?" Darren asked.

"No matter where we go or what we do in life, most of us will always end up in a place like this. Makes you appreciate the little things eh?" James said, with a faraway look in his eyes.

Darren, a young man, knew death was closing in on the man before him, however the words he spoke were correct. We spend very little time in this world, so Darren wanted to ensure he made it worthwhile.

"That's very true, but sure we have loads of time left in us yet," Darren smiled.

"I don't know about me though," James laughed, "Did you hear about Derek O' Brien and Susan?"

"Who?" Darren lied, knowing exactly who James was speaking about.

"The couple who live together just outside of town. He's about your age I think. Anyway, I saw in the newspaper this morning they are missing now too, along with the other poor people who have disappeared recently."

"Oh really? That's crazy isn't it! I hope they are all okay," Darren said, hiding the fact he was responsible for their disappearances and happy with what he had done.

"Me too, my daughter didn't want me coming here on my own today, but who would want to take me," James laughed. "Anyway I better let you get back to your day. It was nice seeing you out and about, it can be tough losing a loved one and I can't imagine what it is like to lose two at the same time. Take care of yourself Darren," James said, and slowly walked away.

Learning his most recent acts had made headlines, Darren suspected a visit from the Gardaí sooner rather than later as his mind raced for a solution on how to deal with any questions they may have for him. He turned and continued on his way to his parent's resting place.

"Hey," Darren said, eyes looking down to the two names etched upon the dark, marble headstone. "I really miss you both. I hope you are at peace and have found it in your hearts to forgive me for the stupidity which caused your deaths."

He listened to the birds chirp their way around him and the traffic passing by in the distance as the warm sun beat its way down upon him without mercy and any effect.

Darren studied every inch of the grave as the

beautiful memories he shared with his parents ran through his mind. He prayed for their forgiveness and understanding.

I just want to be normal and feel something. I thought they could help me achieve that in some way, but I know now they can't, Darren thought, leaning down and adjusting the tiny crucifix resting over the white, grave gravel. *Please don't judge me for this, after all they are the lucky ones, they felt more than I ever will. I came here today to tell you I'm not going to stop, I can't stop! I don't care about dying, this is what I was put here to do, I know that now.*

Darren spent approximately an hour at his parent's side before leaving to go to the supermarket. Driving along Arklow Main Street, he eyed, as he had done so in the past, many individuals, he would enjoy torturing. There would be a lot less questions now however, and more observing.

Walking through the heavy sliding doors, Darren was greeted with a large stand, the headlines on numerous newspapers, both local and national, highlighted his latest deeds. People were missing and the search was on.

He made his way through the aisles picking up various groceries, while smirking to himself, the idea that no one was aware he was the person responsible gave him a sense of satisfaction and excitement, Darren felt untouchable. When he reached the meat counter, he glared at the lumps of animal meat behind the glass, noting how much it resembled human remains. *I bet if it was cooked right, we would even taste very similar if fed to someone who could taste,* Darren reasoned as one of the butchers approached him to attend to his order.

"Do you kill them yourself?" Darren asked, eyes still concentrating on the countless pieces of flesh on display before him.

"No, the carcasses are delivered to us gutted and skinned," the middle-aged man said, placing his hands on his hips.

"I wonder do they make much noise when they are slaughtered, have you ever done it yourself?" Darren continued in his daydream like, daze.

"No, but it's quick and humane," the butcher responded, eyebrows scrunched due to the unusual conversation.

"Humane? Isn't it strange we disguised murder with a less impactful word, so it doesn't sound as bad? Would a person get away with that do you think? I mean if either one of us knew someone who was suffering, or we killed them in a fast manner, would we get away with saying it was the humane thing to do?" Darren replied. In his mind everyone was born an animal. "Oh I'm sorry, listen to me. I was just speaking my random thoughts aloud, don't pay any attention to me, it's been a long day," Darren smiled, turning his eyes to greet the man opposite him.

"No problem at all, so what can I get you?"

Darren placed his order, it didn't matter what was handed out to him over the counter due to experiencing no taste, he could literally eat anything at all, and no gag reflex would react.

He purchased his items, the cashier stating how awful the current news was, and their hope for the missing people to turn up safe and sound, while Darren stood agreeing with the skinned faces attached to him just a few paces away. He did fear he may not have used enough deodorant and there may have been a smell off him, however so far so good. The people he bumped into didn't seem to notice anything.

During the journey home, Darren noticed the Garda car driving a short distance behind him. As he continued, he deviated his attention from the rear-view mirror, to the road before him and back to the mirror again every few seconds, his fists turning white, gripping the steering wheel tightly.

He flicked on the left indicator, then watched the car behind him do the same. Each twinkle of the amber light agitated Darren even more.

Darren parked his van in his driveway and stepped out to greet his official visitors.

Taking a deep breath and exhale, "Officers. How are you?" Darren asked, leaning against the back of the van, arms folded.

"I suppose you've heard about Derek and Susan. Do you mind if we follow you up to the house for a chat?" Garda Cullen asked.

"Not at all, come on in," Darren smiled before turning and opening the gate.

Making his way up the long driveway, Darren

cursed the law officials behind him more than once before his house appeared from behind the treeline. His mind shot back and forth, analysing his movements, his murders and his concealments. There was no way they could know anything, he thought, switching off the engine in front of the dank shed where he carried out many of his heinous experiments.

"So, am I in some kind of trouble here?" Darren quizzed, locking the van behind him.

"No, not at all. We saw you driving past and just wanted to follow up in relation to our investigation into the disappearances. Have you seen and heard anything further?" Garda Cullen asked, as they stepped closer to him.

"The two people from the holiday park, are they still missing? No, I haven't, as you can probably tell I don't get out much," Darren replied.

Glaring at the two individuals in front of him, Darren knew he couldn't keep what he was doing under wraps forever and the Gardaí would eventually want to search all the land close to the disappearances, so he decided to get there before them.

"You know, as I said before, you're welcome to look around if you wish, but I'm one hundred percent sure no one has been on my property," Darren added.

"How would you know for sure, it's a big area right?" Garda Byrne said.

"Trust me, nobody would bother me," Darren

grinned.

"What do you keep over there," Garda Byrne nodded towards the shed.

"Oh, just the usual bits and pieces, here I'll show you," Darren said, walking over to the location which had emitted countless screams. He knew by then he was not going to let them leave, he needed to stay a step ahead.

The two Gardaí followed unaware that the people they were looking for were buried just a short distance away. Decomposition slowly transforming the remains.

Darren unlocked and swung open the large steel door, held out his hand and beckoned them inside, which they did one by one, Garda Cullen remaining near the door.

"See, nothing of interest," Darren said, closing the door behind him.

"Sorry, can you leave that open!" Garda Byrne stated.

"No problem," Darren smiled, "So Derek and Susan now too eh? Do you know what they look like?"

"Yes, we have their pictures on the front page of every newspaper and on the daily news on television. Hopefully someone somewhere has seen them."

"You know they don't look like those pictures anymore," Darren said, knowing that he had the two law officials exactly where he wanted them.

"Wait you've seen them? Where?" Garda Cullen

responded.

"A couple of nights ago. In fact, they aren't far away at all," Darren replied, dead-eyed, stepping closer to the two people in front of him.

"What do you mean?" Garda Byrne replied, also stepping closer to the man who had become intimidating.

Without saying another word, Darren reached for his t-shirt, causing the Gardaí to react by stepping backwards, and slowly revealed the faces of his most recent victims.

"Darren," Garda Byrne said, arm stretched out before him, his other hand on his baton, mouth agape. "Okay, I'm going to need you to get down on your knees!"

Darren turned to Garda Cullen and then back to Garda Byrne with a huge smirk on his face.

"Darren, on the ground, now!" Garda Byrne commanded once again.

Darren lowered his t-shirt and began to walk towards the man in front of him. Both Gardaí removed and wielded their batons while ordering the disturbed individual to submit.

Suddenly, Darren lunged for the Garda in front of him, Garda Byrne swung the baton, which cracked Darren on his right shoulder. His eyes widened noticing that the heavy blow had no effect on Darren as he grabbed the Garda's stab vest with both hands and forced him to the ground.

Knee resting on Garda Byrne's chest, Darren

wrapped his hands around his neck and began to strangle him seconds before another baton was introduced to Darren's upper back area. Turning, Darren witnessed the next swing plummeting towards his temple.

Darren released his grip and stood to his feet, blood now trickling down the left side of his face.

Garda Cullen was amazed that her two forceful impacts didn't bring Darren to his knees while she swung once more with all her might.

Darren blocked the strike with his left forearm and quickly delivered a crushing punch to the woman's jaw, knocking her onto her back and two teeth from her mouth.

"Pointless," Darren grunted, turning to Garda Byrne on the ground behind him, still gaging for air, he ripped the radio from him and smashed it against the wall.

He quickly stepped over to Garda Cullen, who was crawling towards the door, blood spouting from her mouth, her jaw swelling rapidly. Darren also pulled the radio from her and shattered it to pieces.

"Can't have you calling for back up now can I?" Darren said, pacing behind the woman crawling away from him, her crimson body fluid saturating the floor.

Garda Cullen managed to pull herself up onto unsteady legs and began making her way as quickly as possible to the Garda car, Darren close behind her. She knew if she made it to the squad car, she could call for help through the on-board radio and attempt to get away from the dangerous situation.

Hearing Darren's stride quicken, Garda Cullen pushed through the pain and picked up her pace. Noticing how close Darren was to her and gaining, she realised the car was not an option due to the time it would take for her to get into it, so she decided to push towards the road.

Once Darren realised she wasn't going to the car, his attention quickly shot to Garda Byrne back in the shed behind him. If he wasn't careful, he too would escape.

Deciding to let his current target flee, Darren quickly returned to the shed to witness the Garda inside climbing to his feet, using one of the steel pillars Darren used to tie his victims to in the past to aid him.

Darren grabbed the baton left behind by Garda Cullen who had just escaped and beat Garda Byrne between the shoulder blades with it, driving him back down onto the floor.

"You're not getting away that easy!" Darren growled, snatching some left over rope from his previous victims.

Darren hurriedly bound the disorientated man and dragged him over to the work bench.

"Don't make it worse for yourself Darren, just let me go and we'll work this out. Don't ruin your life!" the Garda said, feet dragging the ground beneath him.

Darren leaned the Garda against the bench, his hands firmly tied behind his back.

"Work this out? Who are you trying to convince, me or you?" Darren laughed, before punching the Garda in the face and shoving him up onto the bench.

Darren spun open the handle on the vice beside him, manoeuvred Garda Byrne's head between the steel jaws and clamped them tightly around him.

"Don't do this!" The bound man pleaded, the cold steal pressing firmly against both sides of his temple.

Darren didn't reply and slowly began to spin the handle while watching the Garda's face begin to contort.

Garda Byrne struggled to free his hands from behind his back, however, the wrist restraints were too tight and his body weight resting on top of them didn't help either. He quickly tried to use his legs to push himself out of the vice's grip, but this was rapidly countered by Darren delivering three heavy blows to the Garda's abdomen.

The pressure briskly swelled inside the Garda's head as he begged Darren to stop.

Suddenly Darren felt a little more resistance on the handle and paused. He knew that any further twists would cause the skull to shatter.

"Please..." Garda Byrne wheezed, eyes bulging, vison blurred, blood pouring from his mouth and body jittering about on the work bench.

Darren also noted the small trickle of blood escaping both ears from the man looking up at him in despair.

Darren wrapped his right hand, firmly back around the vice handle and gradually pulled it clockwise. This motion was simultaneously accompanied by loud snaps and crunching as he watched the skin on the Garda's face push together and implode as his head shattered in the vice.

Staring at the limp body before him, Darren knew it wouldn't be long before the place would be overrun with Gardaí and reporters, so he had to act fast.

He loosened the vice, grabbed the knife, the edge of which by then was no stranger to human flesh, and crudely severed the face off the corpse laying awkwardly before him.

After removing the man's identity, Darren left Garda Byrne on bloodied display while he went into his house and fetched two bin bags. Darren placed some food into one and clothing, a needle, thread, the newly acquired face and a hammer into another. He tied the two bags together and draped them over his shoulder. He contemplated racing to the van and driving as far away as possible, however, he assumed checkpoints would be set up in the wider area, and it would be easy to identify him in his vehicle, so he decided to leave the scene on foot and ventured deep into the woodland beside his home to evade capture.

Chapter 12

After walking quite a while and watching the sun beginning to surrender to nightfall, Darren decided to use his current location as his bed for the night.

Thankfully the summer heat had kept the rain at bay for the last number of days, so the embankment he chose for his bedding was dry, not that it would have mattered to Darren, but it was a positive none the less. He placed his bags of supplies beside him and sat down, back resting against the wide trunk of a tall oak tree.

Darren visualised the Gardaí swarming around his property like ants, unaware of the bodies buried beneath their feet. The only regret he had after fleeing from his home, was missing their reactions to the body he left on show for them.

"Speaking of which," Darren smiled, peering into the nearest bin bag to him.

He retrieved the piece of skin and held it up in front of him, the final rays of light piercing through the voids where the eyes, nostrils and mouth should be. Darren lay the remains across his thigh and turned back to the bin bag, from it he pulled the needle and thread.

As he did previously, Darren double threaded the needle and lifted up his t-shirt to reveal the human mural beneath.

He placed Garda Byrne's face against his torso and began to stitch him into place, the satisfaction growing within him each time the tip of the needle passed through the deceased man's flesh into his own. To Darren, he was carrying their last feeling with him in the closest way achievable.

Watching the tiny trickles of blood run down along him, Darren's taste for homicide was by then unstoppable. He just needed the current spotlight on him to dull a little before he could find his next victim.

Earlier that day, while Darren was making his escape, Garda Cullen successfully raised the alarm to the local Garda station. She was instructed to stay away from the property until backup arrived.

Darren's house was cleared first before the brutal discovery was uncovered in the shed at the back of his residence.

A mixture of shock and anger filled the Gardaí taking in the sight of their disfigured colleague, his uniform being his main source of identity. The sight was so disturbing it caused one of them to step outside and release the contents of his stomach.

The area was sealed off for a full forensic examination and soon afterwards the Gardaí noticed the disturbed soil on Darren's land.

They made the decision to dig up the area, the general assumption being something was being concealed beneath it.

After unearthing the bodies, it didn't take long for word to quickly echo around Arklow about the house of horrors lurking within the community.

Pictures of Darren were circulated through all news outlets, both local and national, alongside an appeal for any information on his whereabouts.

After the bodies were removed for a formal post-mortem and the examination was completed, Darren's house was securely boarded up, with a notice put in place to keep away or face prosecution.

The entrance to Darren's land, which was covered in large "Keep Out" notices, attracted a lot of people who wanted to witness where the terrible atrocities was uncovered. Some posed for pictures while others stood in silence, wondering how something so evil could have been carried out so close to home.

"You know they still haven't caught him yet!" One man said to his girlfriend, his arm firmly wrapped around her.

"Well, I hope he is caught soon. Makes you wonder what kind of people are out there doesn't it?" she replied, moving closer to him.

"Very true. It's the perfect place to do it isn't it? So far off the road, I mean we can't even see any sign of the house or shed from here. Just imagine what those poor people went through. I hope they get him and lock him away forever," the man said, staring into the dense treeline, shielding Darren's home.

This was just one of many similar conversations

that took place outside the heavy steel gate barricading access.

The community, although happy the five missing people were found so their families could have some form of closure, was still on high alert due to Darren evading capture.

The news contained some of the horrific details of Darren's crimes, so everyone was on edge, especially when night collapsed over and around Arklow. People were advised to stay indoors as much as possible during the darker hours and ensure their home was secure before going to bed. Further advice broadcast included no individual should walk the streets alone, don't open the door to strangers, keep the outside of your home well-lit, and keep a phone nearby at all times.

The Gardaí carried out more frequent patrols of the area, while Darren's closest neighbours were asked to notify the Gardaí immediately if they noticed any suspicious activity at or near the premises. However, they were strictly informed under no circumstances to approach the man who had brought so much agony and terror to the community.

It didn't take long for the Garda station to receive calls from concerned people, convinced they had spotted Darren lurking in the shadows, most of which were reported at, or very close to Darren's abandoned property.

The Gardaí responded rapidly to every phone call, however, each time it didn't produce any results. They would search the entire area for any sign of Darren and regularly inspect the barricaded home to see if he had returned.

Although in hiding, Darren was still managing to terrorise Arklow and the people who lived there.

Chapter 13

"Okay, time for bed," a woman called into her son's bedroom.

"Just five more minutes Ma I promise," the eleven-year-old called back, while he tried to complete the current level on the computer game he was playing.

Jennifer Robinson was a single mother in her late thirties who lived on the outskirts of Arklow with her son Michael. She worked in the local supermarket and although she never served Darren personally, she remembered him buying his groceries there. When the news broke about him, she couldn't believe it as he always seemed to get on so well with the staff and genuinely seemed like a nice person. Jennifer felt sick when she heard the details of the torture at his premises and like so many other people, she wondered if they were the only ones Darren had gotten his evil hands upon.

It had been almost two months since the Gardaí made the grisly discoveries at Darren's address and there was still no progress on bringing him to justice.

Although people in the area were still stunned by what had happened so close to home, life slowly moved on and Darren was slowly fading into second thoughts.

Jennifer's two-story home was the last of a scattering of houses along the small country road leading from the town. It was just out of the grasp of the street lighting which illuminated Arklow during the dark hours which stretched on longer with each passing autumn day.

"Your five minutes are up, you've school tomorrow!" She called into the room once more, while she folded some clothes in the next bedroom.

"MA!" Michael roared, moments later causing instant panic to explode within his mother.

Jennifer dropped everything and raced to Michael's room to find him standing aside the window peeping out into the night.

"What's wrong?" She asked, stepping over to him. "Michael?" She continued, resting a hand on his shoulder and turning him towards her.

"There is someone out there. I saw a person staring at me," Michael shockingly revealed to his mother.

"Where?" Jennifer quizzed, looking through the glass, greeted with a combination of various shades of darkness and the background light in the room reflexing off it.

"Just by the gate. Do you see?" The child said, clutching tightly onto Jennifer's arm.

Jennifer examined the area as much as she possibly could, however nothing or no one seemed to be lurking outside.

She rationalised Michael must have startled himself

with his reflection or something else in the glass, however she wanted to put his mind at ease.

She was aware Darren was still out there somewhere, so she had to be cautious, while ensuring they both were safe.

"I don't see anyone but I'll go check okay?" Jennifer replied, knowing full well she would not be satisfied unless she did.

"No Mammy don't go out there. What if they get you?" Michael panicked, a tremor in his words, palm rattling on his mother's arm.

"Don't worry, I'll be careful. Plus, I'll have you up here looking out for me," Jennifer smiled, knowing if he saw that no one was there when she went outside, Michael would feel and sleep a lot better. "Here take this, if anything happens dial 999." She added, handing Michael her mobile phone.

After giving him a kiss on the cheek, Jennifer went downstairs and flicked on the outside light as she passed the front door. Although she was rather confident the incident was all in her son's head, Jennifer still wanted to protect herself just in case.

The closest implement she could see which reassembled any form of a weapon was the poker resting beside the glowing blaze in the fireplace. Wrapping her hand around the cold steel, Jennifer made her way to the front door.

She unlocked it and stepped out into night. The bright moonlight combined with the strong glow emitted by the light above her head made visibility easier.

Keeping the blunt, would be weapon, as close to her side as possible, Jennifer turned, looked to the window overhead and smiled to Michael. She didn't want him to see her carrying the poker, thinking it may heighten his fear.

As Jennifer made her way down towards the gate, the first thoughts which sprinted into her mind was, what if someone was there? What if it was Darren? However, she quickly placed a grip around the images of him lurking behind the wall in her mind and brushed them aside.

It was a cool, calm night and when she reached the area Michael claimed to have seen someone surveying the house, thankfully there was no initial clear evidence he was right.

Squeezing the handle tightly, Jennifer opened the gate and stepped out onto the dry gravel beside the road. She was sure to examine left and right before turning and walking back onto her property.

Latching the gate back into position, she stood momentarily embracing the silence. Jennifer then checked the door handles on her car for any sign of tampering, before she made her way back inside, quickly placing the poker back where she found it.

"See, everything is okay," Jennifer smiled, collecting her phone off Michael.

"But there was someone there," Michael said, still peering out towards the road which passed by their house.

"Okay, what did they look like? Was it a man or woman?" Jennifer asked, kneeling beside her son, resting a hand upon his shoulder once again.

"I... I don't know, I couldn't really see that well."

"Well, I checked, and no one is out there, it could have been someone resting against the wall on their way back into town. Or maybe your eyes were only adjusting to the darkness outside," Jennifer explained, still convinced he had let his mind get the better of him. "Don't worry, we're fine, plus I bet you could handle yourself. Come on, time for bed and trust me there is nothing to worry about," Jennifer smiled, giving the young boy a subtle nudge, causing him to smile in return.

Michael glanced out the window once more, relieved to see the area was clear, then went to the bathroom to brush his teeth. Meanwhile, Jennifer pulled the heavy curtains across his window, then lowered the superhero duvet on his bed and switched on the bedside light.

"Are you still warm enough at night?" Jennifer asked Michael when he returned to the room.

"Yeah, I'm fine thanks," he said, climbing into the bed.

"That's good. Okay, sweet dreams. I love you," Jennifer said, dragging the duvet up to her son's chest, kissing him on the forehead.

"Love you too."

Jennifer switched off the overhead light and left the bedroom, leaving the door ajar. She went back into her bedroom to finish folding the clothes she was tending to before Michael's scare. Jennifer smiled to herself, amused at a child's imagination, wondering if she had been like that when she was Michael's age.

Once finished the chore, Jennifer went downstairs, made herself a warm cup of tea, placed more coal into the dulling red embers within the fireplace, and watched television for the remainder of the evening.

The hands on the large wooden clock above the mantelpiece were pointing to twenty minutes to eleven when Jennifer decided to call it a night.

She made her final checks around the house before retiring upstairs to bed.

Staring at the dark ceiling above, her eyes began to swell with tears thinking of the hole left in her when Dermot, her boyfriend, lost his life in a car crash. She remembered receiving the life changing phone at work, hope still rampant within her as she raced to the hospital, convinced the Gardaí and doctors where talking about the wrong person. All of this was dashed when she was asked to identify the twisted, crushed remains on the cold examination table in front of her. Due to the force of the impact, Dermot's spine snapped like a dry twig and his face exploded against the windscreen.

Jennifer didn't have much time to mourn, she needed to be strong for Michael and wasn't comfortable nor willing to break down in front of him. She wanted to go about life as normal as possible when he depended on her the most.

Many nights she found herself lying in bed, head beneath the blankets, crying her heart out, praying she would wake up in the same bed beside Dermot. Hoping it had all been a cruel dream. One hug from him was all it would take to make her pain disappear, but she knew she would never feel his embrace again.

Time made things a little easier, however the piece missing from her could never be replaced.

Jennifer tossed and turned for some time before she managed to reach any form of slumber. It was later that night when Jennifer jumped to life, to what sounded like movement downstairs. She froze in position while listening for any further noise, still unsure if it was a result of being asleep.

After a minute or so passed she spun towards the screen display on the alarm clock beside her bed and watched it flick to 03:37. Taking a prolonged yawn, Jennifer repositioned herself comfortably on her left side and began the process of falling asleep once more, happy that it was her dreams which had gotten the better of her.

Seconds later, she held her breath again hearing another shuffle below her, causing Jennifer to spring to the sitting position on the mattress. She stared towards her bedroom door, examining the edge for any light sources cutting through the darkness from downstairs.

Jennifer's first thought was Michael must be hungry and went down to the kitchen to appease his appetite, although this would be unusual for him.

She climbed from the bed, stepped towards her bedroom door and pulled it open, confident she was going to see the glow of the lights downstairs beating their way through the hall, however she was greeted with thick darkness.

Confused, Jennifer quickly marched towards Michael's room and pushed gently on the door. Her heart raced discovering he was peacefully asleep in his bed.

She pulled the door closed and flicked on the switch beside her to illuminate the hallway and stairs. Jennifer, heart racing, breaths deep, listened a moment to establish if any further noises could be heard from below, however, a dead silence filled the air around her.

Trying to establish if it came from outside or inside the house, as her mind raced through countless possibilities, she made her way to the top of the stairs, her palms becoming more unsteady. Although experiencing high levels of apprehension, there was no way Jennifer was going to go back to bed before making sure everything was okay.

She did consider calling out, "Hello." However, if there was someone in the house, they surely knew she was awake by then, and furthermore she wouldn't be greeting an intruder with such a courteous word.

Eyeing a heavy brass statue at the bottom of the stairs, she decided it would have to do as a weapon to defend herself if anyone advanced from the darkness, which seemed to pulsate slowly just a few steps away from it.

Taking a deep breath, Jennifer placed one bare foot on the worn carpet in front of her, instantly scrunching her eyebrows and biting down on her lip due to the squeak emitted from the wood beneath it. Her impulses wanted to race for the blunt implement, however her body wouldn't allow her.

She stooped over as she slowly made her way downward, to see if she could eye anything out of the ordinary through the banisters.

Jennifer firmly took hold of the statue once it was within reach and then flicked the switch on the inside of the wall opposite her to highlight the entire sitting room. Again, nothing.

There was only one more area to check as the cold air crashed against any bare skin it could while she made her way towards the kitchen.

Raising the statue, ready to introduce it to the head of anyone who had decided to break into her home, Jennifer quickly pressed the switch and stepped into the kitchen to be greeted with an empty room, with nothing seeming to be out of place.

But what was it? She thought to herself as she scanned the area before her. It was at that moment she heard the subtle breeze as the curtain danced to its tune. Jennifer couldn't believe she had forgotten to close the upper piece of the kitchen window and kicked herself for being so silly in the build-up to finding the cause of her concerns.

Exhaling a deep sigh of relief, Jennifer placed the

statue onto the table and pulled the window closed and locked it, still sure she had examined the entire house before bed but put her oversight down to a slip of the mind.

Before she returned to bed, Jennifer double checked on Michael, who was still sound asleep, then she lay back down, happy she went to see what was causing the noises from downstairs.

The following morning, Jennifer made breakfast as usual before calling Michael. While moving back and forth from the sink she continued to grin at the window in front of her due to it causing her to strategically navigate her way through the house a few hours before.

"Morning sleepy head," Jennifer smiled, watching Michael step into the kitchen and sit down at the table. "Did you sleep okay?"

"Yeah I did," Michael replied, pouring himself some orange juice.

The answer made Jennifer happy following the scare he had the previous night, little did he know Jennifer had experienced her own fright herself.

"Good. Don't forget your jacket today, they are saying a storm is coming in later," Jennifer instructed, after hearing the news earlier that morning.

Once they finished their breakfast, Jennifer drove Michael to school and then made her way to work.

Jennifer really liked her job, the fact she could start her shift after the morning school run and finish in time to pick Michael up afterwards really made life a lot easier.

The wind and heavy downpours swept over the country in the early afternoon and the forecast said it was going to last through the night until early the following morning.

Jennifer wasted no time driving to pick Michael up once her shift was over as she didn't want him to stand too long waiting for her in the harsh elements.

Once home, Michael sat at the kitchen table and began his homework whilst Jennifer lit the fire, then began preparing their dinner.

The pair enjoyed dinner together before Michael returned to finish the rest of his schoolwork as the wind and rain wildly assaulted the windows beside him.

One rule Jennifer had was no computer games were allowed before he was finished, even if she did help him along the way with any revision he found too difficult.

Darkness crept around the house when Michael went upstairs to play games before it was bedtime. He couldn't help but peer out through the water running down the pane of glass beside him towards the area he was convinced someone had been staring up at him the night previous. To his relief, no one was there.

Meanwhile, Jennifer watched television, while enjoying a warm cup of tea when suddenly her attention was drawn to the loud alarm and flashing amber lights beating off the curtains from outside.

"Stay here," Jennifer said, as she was met in the hallway by Michael, equally confused by what was causing the piercing commotion.

"What's wrong?"

"Don't worry, I'm going to check now, but stay inside," Jennifer explained as she made her way over to the front door, the poker from the fireplace in her grasp once again.

Her first thought was someone was trying to steal her car as she took a deep breath and slowly unlocked the front door to the house.

Ensuring Michael was at a safe distance, Jennifer opened the door slightly and peaked out as the rain instantly splashed against her face.

It was difficult to see, and the bright flashing lights didn't help.

After analysing the area as best as possible, Jennifer pulled the door aside and stepped out into the elements, senses on high alert for any signs of intrusion on, or around her property.

She clicked the button on her car keys which deactivated the alarm and walked around the vehicle, joined by Michael seconds later.

"I told you to stay inside," she said, as the rain and wind continued to violently make their presence known.

Michael didn't reply, he just felt safer near his mother.

After quickly checking the car and watching the wind shake the suspension with each forceful howl,

Jennifer assumed that was what caused the alarm to squeal to life.

"It was the wind," Jennifer said, closing the door behind her, ushering Michael to the warm fire. "Sooner it's gone the better," she smiled, rubbing her hands together, the water still running down her face.

After enjoying the comforting warmth radiating from the fire, Jennifer stood and went upstairs to the bathroom to fetch a large towel.

After drying themselves, Michael and Jennifer spent the rest of the evening in the sitting room watching television. Jennifer was on the edge of her seat, waiting for the alarm to wail once again with each gust, however she was thankful the car remained silent.

Following Michael going to bed, Jennifer decided to have an early night herself.

Lying under the comfort of her duvet, Jennifer enjoyed listening to the rain and wind beat against her home, while praying she wouldn't have to leave the cosy mattress to switch off the car alarm.

At least I know it's working I suppose, Jennifer smiled to herself as she pointed her toes towards the foot of the bed, relishing a long stretch, she yawned and turned onto her side, pulling the duvet tighter around her, before drifting off to sleep soon afterwards.

The rain and wind became fiercer as the night wore on, causing the trees in the surrounding area to groan louder under the strain.

It was after three o' clock when Jennifer was awoken from her peaceful slumber by a commotion which seemed to be coming from the same floor she was on.

Sitting rigid on the mattress, she heard it again, sounds of what seemed to be someone moving about in the opposite room. She assumed Michael got up to use the bathroom, however found it unusual that she didn't see any indication of lights switched on or doors opening and closing.

Noticing the noises, which she was sure were coming from Michael's bedroom were not ceasing, Jennifer climbed from the bed and made her way to her bedroom door.

She turned on the light, thankful the electricity supply had not been interrupted by the storm and stepped out into the hallway.

"Michael?" Jennifer called out, walking over to his bedroom door, the disturbance within continuing.

Not wasting any time, Jennifer pushed open the door and flicked the switch beside her.

Her jaw almost hit the ground beneath her as Jennifer's blood ran cold taking in the sight of her son struggling wildly in the grasp of an intruder in their home.

"MICHAEL!" Jennifer roared stepping closer, her face pale from shock.

"That's far enough!" A man's voice hissed from beneath the black hood concealing a portion of his face.

He had a firm grip on Michael with his right arm and then he raised his left hand to reveal a hammer and placed the head of it against Michael's temple.

"Please don't hurt him. I'll do anything," Jennifer said, panic coursing through her, watching the fear in her son's wide eyes as the dirt ridden hand covered his mouth, preventing his calls for help.

"That's the plan," the man replied, an evil grin the only distinguishing thing visible. "They thought I was gone. They thought this town was safe, but I have more work to do," the man continued raising his hand holding the weapon towards the top of his head.

Jennifer looked on in terror, her mind being bombarded by fear and helplessness.

In one rapid motion the intruder pulled back the hood to reveal a familiar face to Jennifer, it was Darren.

Her hope quickly diminished remembering the terrible crimes he carried out and the viciousness associated with them. Now this monster had her beloved son in his grip as Darren repositioned the hammer beside the young boy's head once more.

"Darren! Please let him go. You can do whatever you want to me but please don't hurt him," Jennifer begged, listening to her son mumbling in fear.

"Shut up you!" Darren growled, thumping the cold steel against Michael's head to demonstrate his authority.

Jennifer moved closer, the sight of her child being struck was sickening to her.

"And what exactly do you think you are going to do?" Darren asked, hammer stretched out before him towards Jennifer. "You're going to do exactly what I say, or I'll crack his head. Do you understand me?"

"Do... You... Understand?" Darren said once again in a firmer tone.

"Yes," Jennifer replied, eyes swelling, realising the hopeless situation she and her son found themselves in.

"Good. Now... downstairs," Darren instructed, walking towards her, ensuring he had a tight hold of Michael.

Walking down the stairs, Jennifer's eyes raced for any solution to the situation she and Michael were in. She considered reaching for the same statue she used as a weapon the night previous, however it was too risky with her son's life in Darren's evil hands.

"In there," Darren pointed towards the sitting room door. "Stand in the centre of the room."

Jennifer did as ordered, as she watched Darren shove the small table out of the way with his foot to give her more space.

Jennifer didn't take her eyes off Michael's, which were by then pouring tears down the back of Darren's gritty hand, "Why us?"

"Why not? You were an easy choice," Darren grinned. "It was effortless getting to you."

"What do you mean?" Jennifer quizzed.

"Well, you are out of the way here. I watched you for some time, it was easy to pop the window open, so I climbed in and got familiar with the place. I bet you didn't even check for damage afterwards eh? Then earlier, I simply set off the car alarm so you would come running out to check on it, which gave me the opportunity to slip inside," he stated. "You know I almost wanted to grab you a few nights ago when you came out to the gate looking for me. But that would have been a risky move, now that I have him, I know you'll do whatever I ask."

Jennifer realised Michael had in fact seen someone outside the house the night he called her to his bedroom. She also knew it was Darren in their home the night she heard the movements downstairs.

"You don't have to do this," Jennifer said, the details of Darren's murders running through her mind.

"You make it sound like I am a bad person," Darren spat back.

"I'm sorry, I'm not saying that. I just mean we can resolve this another way, that's all," Jennifer replied, hands out in front of her trying to calm the situation before it escalated any further, her eyes focused back on her son.

"Enough of your nonsense. Here you'll need this," Darren snarled, swapping the hammer to his right hand and reached into his hoodie pocket with the left.

Seconds later, Darren revealed a knife which he had taken from the block of knives beside the window in Jennifer's kitchen and tossed it to her feet.

Confused as to why he would give her a weapon,

Jennifer leaned over and picked it up.

"I bet you'd love to sink that in right here wouldn't you?" Darren asked, pointing to the centre of his chest.

If the truth was known, the moment she grasped the handle, Jennifer visualised racing towards him and stabbing him multiple times in any available areas she could in order to protect Michael. However, she couldn't gamble the risk of her son getting caught in the violent crossfire. She felt useless and knew Darren was in control.

"What do you want me to do with this?" Jennifer asked, the glint of the blade catching her eye.

"I want you to cut your left forearm open and show your son what we are all made of," Darren said, his unblinking glare fixed firmly upon the dismayed woman.

"What?" She replied, praying she had misheard him.

"If you don't, I am going to take it from you and stick it into his eye," Darren responded, his glaze even more intense.

"Mammy don't do it," Michael cried out.

"It's okay... everything will be alright," Jennifer smiled to her son trying to ease the fear stinging through him.

Hoping the act would save Michael, Jennifer placed the tip of the blade against her soft skin, then applied pressure.

Taking a deep breath, Jennifer pulled the handle

down towards her wrist, the blood instantly pouring from it to the floor beneath her. The pain was excruciating but the fight to save Michael helped Jennifer hold herself together as best as possible while she watched her skin separate behind the knife.

"Very good. Now the side of your face and don't go easy this time," Darren instructed, relishing in the sight before him.

Confident that arguing or pleading would do no good, Jennifer raised the edge of the blade and pressed it firmly against her right cheek looking towards her son.

She pulled on the handle once again and the blade sliced deep into her flesh. The immense pain caused Jennifer to stop momentarily and cry out as she lowered the knife.

"Come on, you can do better than that. Keep going!" Darren demanded, his cruddy hand firmly gripping Michael's neck.

The wounds were already causing paralysing, intense, pulsating pain, which radiated around the areas they were inflicted. However, fighting her natural impulses, Jennifer reintroduced the cold steel to the initial slash on her face and pulled fast, deep and hard which resulted in a huge, wide gash on her face.

Jennifer instantly pressed her hands against her severed flesh to try and ease the agony eating its way through her, but it was useless.

"Leave Mammy alone," Michael roared, tossing

about within Darren's grasp.

"Stay still. If you love her so much you'll shut up or I'll go over and finished the job," Darren threatened, squeezing Michael's neck tighter.

Had this been the first time Darren had witnessed someone in so much agony he would have asked Jennifer to explain what she was going through; however it was pointless. He tried that process many times in the past and achieved no satisfaction, their reactions were the closest to pain he was ever going to get.

"Pull it together. We're not done yet," Darren spat across the room to Jennifer.

The slashed woman wanted the pain to be over, but it was clear Darren wasn't going to allow her any respite.

"Let him go and I'll do whatever you want!" Jennifer cried out, keeping her composure as much as she possibly could.

"It doesn't work like that! Do you think you are in any position to be giving me orders? I will snap his neck in front of you and before you even know what has happened, I will bury this in your face," Darren snarled, holding the blunt hammer out in front of him once again. "Now, run the blade along the sole of your foot and if I for one moment think you are going easy, he dies!" Darren confirmed.

Jennifer didn't hesitate for one second and carved a huge cavity into her foot. Unknown to her, Darren was making her carry out the act so she couldn't get away too easy.

Darren watched her lower the injured foot delicately back onto the floor, the blood pouring from her numerous wounds pooling on the carpet beneath them. He analysed her expressions and noted her will to self-inflict hurt to prevent her son going through the same thing.

"Now him!" Darren said, releasing Michael and pushing him towards her, after what seemed like an eternity staring at Jennifer.

"No way, leave him out of this," Jennifer quickly snapped back, gripping the knife tighter in her hand.

"Cut him or I will!" Darren roared.

Jennifer couldn't believe what she was hearing, there was no way she was going to harm Michael in any way.

"You're sick. Leave him out of this,"

"Slice him open!" Darren instructed, stepping closer, he wanted to see the effect it would have on Michael both mentally and physically as his mother carved into him.

Jennifer paused a moment as Michael stood awestruck at his mother's injuries and the ultimatum put to her by Darren. No matter what, there was no way she could bring herself to hurt her son.

"Run Michael," Jennifer screamed, looking at the despair in his eyes.

Michael turned and raced for the sitting room door, while Jennifer lumbered her way towards Darren with the knife.

Reacting quickly, Darren flung the hammer at Michael, connecting against his head with a cruel, loud thud, dropping the child to the ground instantly.

Jennifer swiped at Darren in a feeble attempt, however Darren easily dodged her attack and returned with a firm punch to her nose, immediately flattening it across her face, dropping her to the floor.

Without any hesitation Darren climbed upon her and rained down a torrent of heavy, closed fists. Each one ricocheting her head against the floor.

Jennifer tried her best to fight back, however it had no effect on Darren.

Lifting his right arm as high as possible, he delivered a thunderous blow to Jennifer's jaw, spinning her head towards Michael who was lying motionless just a short distance away, the crimson fluid rapidly escaping from his head.

Darren then dug his thumbs into Jennifer's mouth. Placing them on each side, he began to pull as hard as he possibly could, while she trashed about underneath his body weight. Darren quickly adjusted his grip and placed as many fingers as possible either side of her mouth and pulled with all his strength, causing her to scream in agony.

Eyeing the tissue painstakingly stretch to its limit, it then began to tear and bleed, before Darren punched her once more rendering her semiconscious.

Darren stood and walked over to the hammer lying beside Michael. He picked it up and paused over the boy, studying the large crack in the side of his head. Darren knew it wouldn't be long before life escaped Michael's body, if it hadn't already, so he swung the hammer downwards, smashing the boy's head even further.

Darren then leaned over, grabbed the child's arm and dragged him back over to his mother, who was still trying to deal with the pulsating agony. He tossed Michael's limp body across her and kneeled beside the pair.

"You where stupid to even think I was going to let either of you go," Darren said, before collecting the knife Jennifer lost in her tussle with him.

He pointed the tip of the blade towards her left eye and without a moment's thought, plunged it deep into her skull, killing Jennifer instantly.

"I would give anything to feel what you just did, even just a little," Darren sighed, looking towards Jennifer's corpse.

Darren didn't care about covering his tracks at that stage because the Gardaí knew who had committed the crimes he carried out and once they discovered Jennifer and Michael, they would surely put two and two together.

Darren reached into his pocket and took out a knife he had concealed on him the whole time. He brought his own because he felt it would be sharper than any he would find in the house.

Not wasting any time, he began to remove the skin from Jennifer's face to add it to the collection of expressions he already had attached to him.

Once he cut around the perimeter, Darren placed a firm boot on Jennifer's flowing hair to stop her head rising when he pulled the flesh from her.

Darren knew that Jennifer would be the last face he could stitch to his torso due to space constraints, however he decided to remove Michael's and bring it with him either way, to have it as a memento of his deeds.

Happy with his work, Darren checked Jennifer's kitchen for all available food and tossed it into a bin bag he found beneath the sink. He folded both faces, placed them into his pocket, then he switched off all the lights and left the house through the front door.

Chapter 14

After leaving Jennifer's home, Darren made his way back to his own house. Unknown to the Gardaí and the local community, he had returned to the horrid location sometime after the grim discoveries at the area were uncovered, once he felt the interest in him had passed. He used the hammer he took with him the day he left the premises to smash one of the heavy boards from the windows to gain access.

During his time hiding in the vast woodland, Darren lived off the food he had taken with him the day he escaped, and once he ran out, he lived off the land as best he could.

Climbing through the window at the rear of the property, Darren made his way to the empty sitting room.

The Gardaí had taken every single item from the building for forensic purposes, this also prevented any individuals trying to steal a souvenir from a notorious crime scene. The electricity supply was also cut from the home once it was cleared.

Darren stepped over to the fireplace and introduced a flame to the collection of twigs he had placed within it. He wasn't worried about lighting a fire at such an hour because the darkness would conceal the smoke.

Darren removed his hoodie and sat on the floor. He then pulled up his t-shirt and leaned back against the wall.

Looking down towards the faces stitched to himself, Darren could still remember their cries due to each pulse of pain injecting its way through them.

Darren turned and reached into the hoodie laying on the floor beside him and from it retrieved the faces he cut from his most recent victims.

He laid Michael's on the floor and placed Jennifer's skin on his thigh and watched the shadows cast from the fire dance about upon it.

An idea crossed Darren's mind. He had stitched other people's skin to his own knowing it would always be impossible to feel anything. However, he wondered what effect it would have if he removed some skin from two or more people, switched it around and secured it onto the opposite person. He knew when skin grafts were carried out in hospital and healed people experience sensations from it. However, if he swapped the skin and immediately inflicted pain, would it be felt?

These delusional thoughts peaked his interest and it was something he was determined to experiment with. In the meantime, however, Darren fetched the needle and thread, then fixed the final face in position, making the total number attached to him, five.

Soon afterward Darren drifted off to sleep.

His dreams were a mixed concoction. At times he

dreamt his parents were still alive and he had not let his obsession get the better of him. These were nice memories and he wished occasionally that his parents were still with him, however he knew they would want nothing to do with him after what he had become. At other times, Darren dreamed of the injuries he inflicted on his victims and often dreamt of new victims. During some of these night fantasies he didn't suffer from his condition and was able to feel things just like everyone else. Darren would awake and momentarily believe his dreams were true, however reality would never allow too much time to pass before hitting him hard.

The following morning Darren awoke after experiencing a similar slumber where he had his missing senses, and as always, the numbness of his condition didn't take long to make itself known.

Glancing towards the dead fire beside him, Darren stood and walked over to one of the boarded up windows, pulling back the curtains to reveal his reflection.

The images of the faces looking back at him pleased him. However, his skin looked like everyone else's even though it wasn't. Darren decided this feature had to change. He was happy with his evolution and wanted to use his body as a statement.

He turned and picked up the knife and stood back in front of the pane of glass.

Without a moment's thought, Darren began

cutting into his flesh. He cut around his face, down his forearms and across his upper chest. Pleased with the numerous open wounds, he tossed the knife to the floor and examined the reflection before him.

The blood flowed but nothing more. He couldn't feel it leaving his body. As always, it was a surreal experience.

Not having the ability to feel did not affect Darren's intelligence however. He was very much aware that he could die from extensive blood loss just like anyone else, so be began stitching the pieces of skin back together.

Darren began with each forearm, ensuring the sides of the flesh were pulled together fully he moved onto his face and it was here he decided he didn't need to be precise. In Darren's mind, following his first kill, he had changed and grown so much compared to the young man he was before with no obvious direction in life. However, now on the path he felt he needed to travel, Darren wanted his appearance to reflect whom he developed into.

Pushing the needle through the sliced skin on his right cheek, Darren grabbed the flesh and stretched it beyond the wound at an angle towards the corner of his mouth and began to stitch, as the blood continued to flow down his face.

Next, he pinched the skin on his forehead, dragged it together as unevenly as possible, while still preventing blood loss, and fixed it into position. He stitched the smaller nicks as they were. Finally, he tended to the large gash he created on his lower left jaw by grabbing the skin and pulling it beyond the actual cut, towards his neck and secured it in place.

Happy, Darren used his t-shirt to wipe away the access body fluid from his reconfigured face and took in the sight.

Looking back at him, Darren saw an image of progression and the way his face was now contorted, an expression of what pain would possibly look like on him.

As the morning sunlight began to retreat behind the thick clouds making their way across the sky, Darren turned his attention to his next victims. He knew he wouldn't be long before Jennifer and Michael's bodies were found, so attention would quickly turn back to the property he was currently hiding within.

Darren put his hoodie back over his shoulders and then rummaged through the food he stole from Jennifer's kitchen.

After getting some nourishment into his stomach, Darren climbed from his house, through the broken window, out into an overcast day.

Staring towards the shed, flashbacks of the torture and screams from within it washed over him. Darren turned his eyes towards the general area where he buried the bodies on his property, he would have loved to have seen the reaction on their faces when the Gardaí dug them up and witnessed what he did to the corpses, but he knew now wasn't the time for reminiscing. Darren had to move fast to be able to carry out his next experiment. But before he did, he needed to get some supplies, specifically more thread as he used most of it to reconfigure and secure his face to the grim display it now was, and some restraints.

Darren knew there was a tiny, family run shop, situated beside a pharmacy on the outskirts of town which sold everything from food, household fuel, toiletries to general DIY equipment. That would be his best option to resupply.

So, without wasting anymore time, Darren retreated into the woods beside him and made his way towards Arklow using the treeline to hide his movements as much as possible while he moved through it just a short distance from the road.

When he reached the edge of the woods, Darren could see the rooftops of the town in the distance, he would have to travel the last piece of his journey through open fields.

While stepping through the undergrowth, he heard several vehicles pass by, each time he made sure he was out of sight. He didn't want anyone to know he had returned to the area before he studied what results swapping someone's skin to another would produce.

Darren swung his eyes left and spotted the small forecourt which the shop and pharmacy sat upon. There were people coming and going so he had to be extra careful to ensure he didn't get caught.

Mud up to his knees, Darren crept through the thick grass towards the area behind the shop, where he was sure he would find everything he needed.

Hearing the soggy ground give beneath him, he assumed his feet were cold, however he never once felt what that was like, but he did know if they were wet and left them that way they would deteriorate very quickly. The thought of which brought a smile to his twisted face due to what he had done to other parts of his body recently and further into the past.

Darren reached the fencing behind the shop without any issue and began surveying the area. He decided that the easiest way he could steal what he needed, was to get everyone out of the building, and the best way to do that was to set off the fire alarm.

Thankfully, the rear of the premises seemed quiet and the barrier in front of him was not high.

The space at the back of the property was used as a storage area. Darren viewed cylinders of gas, bags of coal, empty pallets, waste bins, and a small metal container. From what he could tell, it was a shared space between the two businesses.

Knowing he would not get a better opportunity, Darren made one final check, quickly climbed the wooden fencing and made his way over to the door at the rear of the shop. He could hear the world passing by on the opposite side of the buildings, but all was calm where he was, a situation he hoped would remain that way over the next number of minutes.

Darren tried the door handle. Locked. He sighed, knowing the longer he was out in the open, the higher the risk of getting caught.

Thankfully, the wooden door was very much past its prime and the shop owners had a steel shutter overhead which he assumed they pulled down after business hours, which may have contributed to why they didn't replace it when the time came.

Darren forced his palm against the frosted pane of glass and witnessed a tiny crack emerge around the edge between it and the wooden frame.

He repositioned himself and placed his two hands flat against the window in the centre of the old door. Darren began to slowly push while glancing about the area to confirm he was still going about his business unnoticed.

A loud crunch followed by a smash echoed about the area moments later as Darren ejected the glass from the door.

Eyeing the break glass unit for the fire alarm a short distance away, Darren wasted no time cracking the side of his fist against it which instantly caused a thunderous wail to ricochet throughout the building. He waited and listened as the people from inside made their way to the fire assembly point located a safe distance away at the front of the building.

Satisfied enough time had passed, Darren unlocked the door and made his way inside.

He stepped into a tiny room at the rear of the shop and was greeted by another door before him. Darren slowly opened and made his way through it, where he found himself behind the till and counter. Not caring for the money in front of him, Darren quickly looked around the area to see that he was alone. He turned his eyes towards the large window at the front of the shop, through which he witnessed the customers and staff gathering at the designated area, confusion etched across their faces, each looking for an answer to what was happening.

Darren knew he had to be quick, so he grabbed one of the baskets from the stack to his left and began to make his way around the aisles as fast as he could, while occasionally checking the front of the building to ensure no one had joined him.

Darren gathered numerous items which included, needles, thread, rope, duct tape, tinfoil trays, a small axe, a torch, batteries, and some general food items. Satisfied, Darren tossed over numerous shelves, the piercing alarm cloaking the sound, to conceal what he had stolen. Darren was sure if the Gardaí knew exactly what was taken it wouldn't take them long to trace the break in to him. With the shop in turmoil, Darren then raced back behind the counter towards the door he had broken in through.

Meanwhile the continuing alarm caused the people in the pharmacy to come out through the side exit to see what was going on and to Darren's surprise the door had not fully closed back into position. Without a second thought he darted inside.

Moving quickly through the shelves, Darren

snatched a handful of syringes, some medical tubing, and packets of sleeping tablets.

"Hey, what are you doing?" A voice called from the opposite side of the building.

Turning, Darren eyed one of the staff members who stayed behind, racing towards him.

Darren, although he would have enjoyed it, didn't want to engage in the confrontation, because if he did, the others from outside may have gotten involved and he would be quickly overwhelmed. So Darren ignored him and ran for the exit, knocking over everything he could in the process.

The man gave chase but stopped when he saw Darren hop over the fence behind the premises and make good his getaway.

The fire brigade arrived a short time later, after the staff member from the pharmacy went to the assembly point to tell everyone what happened. The Gardaí were called and both the staff and the customers of the two businesses were instructed to remain outside.

It didn't take long for the emergency services to establish there was no fire and discover the broken window and break glass unit at the rear of the shop. They relayed this information to the Gardaí when they arrived at the scene.

The Gardaí searched and secured both buildings, then they combed the adjoining area for any sign of the intruder reported to them, however Darren was long gone. They took a statement off the individual who told them he didn't get a good look at the person he chased away and examined the door which he used to break into the shop. The Gardaí also asked the managers of each premises if they noticed any obvious items missing, however due to the mess Darren created, the task was not possible at the time. Before leaving, the Gardaí told everyone to report any suspicious activity, gave some advice to both managers on upgrading their security and left to carry out further patrols in the area.

Meanwhile, Darren made his way back towards his home, happy he had gotten away safely and satisfied with the items he collected.

Walking through the woodland hugging his property, Darren turned his thoughts to the skin swapping experiment he wanted to carry out. He didn't care much for being discreet anymore because it wouldn't be much longer until the stiff bodies of his last victims were found. Darren needed to locate the next people to experiment with fast, before the Gardaí came kicking in the door to the house he was hiding within.

Reaching home, Darren scouted the property to make sure it was safe before making his way inside. He placed the basket on the floor and then stuffed some food into his mouth.

It was still a few hours until nightfall and Darren decided he would need to strike once darkness swept across the country.

Darren also elected to go to the nearest source of

skin to his property, there was no time to hand pick the perfect targets. The closest living neighbours to him would have to do.

Planning ahead, Darren fetched the basket of his newly acquired supplies and went back outside. He knew if the Gardaí had even the slightest suspicion he was back, his house would be the first place they would search, and he didn't want to lose the items he needed.

Once he hid them, Darren returned to the confines of his house, sat on the floor and allowed his mind to wander.

He felt he had grown since he first began to try to understand what pain was, and the effects it had on the body. Initially he thought words would help him gain a better appreciation for what it's like to experience hurt inflicted on the human body, however Darren realised their reactions to what he did to them would have to be enough. But his latest idea gave him food for thought. He needed to see how people would act once he attached someone else's skin to an area from which he removed theirs.

He knew he wouldn't be able to study his specimens over a long period of time and the initial pain would more than likely be the only thing they would feel, however he had to do it. Darren needed to feed off the reactions he would witness.

He leaned back against the wall behind him, his twisted, stitched face displaying a smirk as he thought of the satisfaction he was going to experience later that day. The only question was how many people he would be able to experiment on.

Chapter 15

As the heavy darkness collapsed around Arklow, it brought with it an icy chill and a slow drizzle.

Darren wasted no time and went outside to the area where he hid the items he stole earlier that day.

From the basket Darren retrieved the torch and loaded it with batteries, he then fetched the small axe, the needles and thread, and a piece of rope. He stuffed all but the axe into the front pocket on his hoodie which still had the blood-stained knife within it, and he began making his way to the closest occupied property to his home.

Darren elected to walk straight down his driveway, crossed the road and leapt into the field on the opposite side and began stepping towards the closest, occupied residence.

As he walked through the saturated grass, Darren needed at least two people to carry out his next study. Being a recluse, Darren had little or no idea who lived around him. Even before he began his murderous ways, he kept to himself, it was the way he liked it.

Darren knew he was taking a risk as he didn't know the internal layout of the location or how many people lived within the building, however, the urgency of the situation meant he had no time, he needed to act as quickly as possible before the Gardaí caught up with him once again.

Darren was making his way towards the bungalow when he passed behind the charred remains of the building where he carried out his first kill. Not even an ounce of sorrow washed over him as he thought of how Mary's skin must have charred and burned as the fire he had set engulfed the old woman. Darren had come a long way since breaking into her home that evening and the community still believed it was a cruel accident which took her life.

Darren had stirred up immense fear within the locality and he wasn't finished yet as the glow of Arklow's street lighting beat against the night sky in the distance.

As the rain became heavier, Darren eyed light cutting through the darkness closer to him. It was being emitted through the windows of the house he had focused his devious attentions on.

Darren flicked off the torch and crept over to the ditch between him and the property he was about to invade.

Looking around the area, Darren didn't see any sign of a dog, something of which he would need to take care of in order to mask his entry to the premises. His goal was to get as close as he could to the house before anyone knew he was there.

Happy it was safe to proceed, Darren stepped through the drain in front of the ditch, which was full of dank, stagnant water and pushed his way through the mixture of briars, nettles and branches into the back garden not caring for the further cuts caused to any of his exposed flesh.

Darren checked his pocket to make sure he hadn't lost anything along the way and moved to the window which the light was being projected from.

Glancing up, he spotted the top pane was slightly open which he assumed was an effort to help battle the condensation running along the inside of the glass.

Peeping into the room, Darren saw an empty kitchen with cutlery in the sink containing the remains of evening's dinner.

Darren turned his eyes towards the doorway which led into the adjoining sitting room and a massive smile burst open upon his disfigured face.

Inside, Darren saw an old couple huddled comfortably together on the large sofa watching television beside a roaring fire.

Perfect! Darren thought, scanning the window and the items behind it to see if he could quietly gain entry. However, unfortunately, the sink was directly below it, so he would make a lot of noise using that route.

Darren decided he would need to get one of them to come to the door so he could overpower them and use the situation to control the other person. This tactic worked well in the past and should be easier this time round due to their age.

Before he ducked down below the window sill, Darren witnessed his monstrous reflection looking back as him. To Darren the new face he created for himself, represented his emotional turmoil, because although he was immune to physical torment, he still felt the disappointment of not being able to do so.

He made his way over to the door to his right and tried the handle.

To Darren's surprise the couple had left their home unlocked, but he still preferred to get one of the elderly pair firmly in his grasp before beginning the flesh removal.

Darren stood and tapped his knuckles against the door in front of him and waited.

Inside the elderly gentleman looked towards the woman in his embrace, both confused as to why someone was at the back of their property.

Darren continued to rap lightly on the wooden door.

"We must not have heard the front door," the old man rationalised, standing up upon his rickety legs, and fetched his walking stick from beside the sofa. It was the only reason he could think of why someone was knocking on the back door rather than just breaking in. However, he still had his guard up. "Stay here love, I'll go see who it is."

Reaching the kitchen, he fixed his eyes on the only barrier between him and whomever was outside it.

He walked around the kitchen table and reached his withered, veiny, hand out and switched on the light over the door to reveal Darren's silhouette standing on the opposite side of the frosted glass.

"Hello?" The elderly man called, eyes glancing to the lock, realising he forgot to engage it after the couple finished their dinner.

The knocking stopped.

"Who's there?" The man called, stepping closer to the door.

There was no reply.

Frustrated, he walked over and opened the door to be greeted by the hellish sight of Darren's face glaring back to him.

Before the man's eyes and mouth could widen fully, Darren lunged towards him and quickly overpowered the feeble attempt to shrug him away. Darren spun the old man on his heels, wrapped his arm around the man's shoulders and searched his pockets, pulling from them a mobile phone. Darren then placed the edge of the small axe to his temple.

"Is everything okay?" The old woman called from the sitting room.

"Get out, don't come in here," her restrained husband yelled, terror rattling through his voice.

"She better not leave or I will hunt her down and smash her face in, in front of you," Darren said in a low, clipped tone.

"What's wrong? Who was it?" The old woman asked, rounding the kitchen door to see what all the commotion was about.

She froze, seeing the intruder holding the weapon to her husband's head and the panic in his eyes as he roared to get out once again.

"Don't you go anywhere!" Darren spat across the room, "Phone?"

"What?" The woman asked in a rattling tone.

"Your mobile phone. He had one so I'm sure you do too,"

The frail woman looked towards her husband and then back to Darren. His face causing her stomach to churn.

"PHONE!" Darren yelled, causing the woman to jolt in front of him.

Without saying a word, the woman reached into her cardigan and placed the phone onto the kitchen table.

"Okay, now sit over there," Darren instructed, pointing the axe towards the chair on the opposite side of the table.

She did as she was told as Darren pushed forward with her husband firmly under his control.

Darren placed the phone he took from his captive beside the other and with one vicious blow to each, he smashed them to pieces.

"You sit here," Darren said, pulling out a chair across from the old woman and shoving the old man downward.

"What do you want?" The woman asked, still in disbelief at what was unfolding in front of her.

Darren gave no explanation as he reached for the pocket on his hoodie and from it retrieved the rope.

He proceeded to secure the man's ankles to the legs of the chair and then pulled the rope up and around his torso and the back of the chair several times. Once satisfied, Darren cut off the waste and used it to carry out the same procedure on the woman facing them.

"Names?" Darren asked, standing upright, tossing the remainder of the rope onto the kitchen table.

The old couple looked to one another, each more terrified than the expression portrayed in front of them.

"Names," Darren asked once more, releasing a deep sigh.

"Elizabeth," the woman answered, a tear cutting its way down along her cheek.

"And you?" Darren asked, turning his torn, stitched face to his left.

"Fra... Frank," passed the man's lips as he looked on helplessly.

"Nice to meet you both," Darren said, reaching into the front pocket on his hoodie to retrieve the needles and thread, the knife and placed them between the pair.

Darren stood at the head of the table and pulled down the hood covering his head to reveal the full extent of his hideous, self-inflicted features, a canvas of which made him almost unrecognisable as human.

"Take anything you want but please don't hurt us," Elizabeth said, her eyes still fixed on her husband who was pushing against the rope to see if it budge.

Darren witnessed similar pleas in recent times and concluded people will offer anything to prevent any sensation of pain, whereas, he would give anything to feel it.

"The only thing in this house you can offer me is you," Darren replied, as he stepped behind Elizabeth and reached down for the blood-stained blade he brought with him. "Tell him you love him!"

Tears flowed down Elizabeth's wrinkled skin as images of the man standing over her stabbing the infested blade deep into her flooded her mind, "I love you Frank."

"I love you too. Please, whatever you have in mind, do it to me, leave her alone," Frank instructed, trying his utmost to loosen the rope holding him in position. He knew there was no way it was going to end well, realising who it was carrying out the horrible act in their home.

The old couple had heard about the gruesome things Darren did, however they thought he had either died or long left the area.

"You're both going to go through the same experience, no need to worry about that," Darren said, placing the tip of the knife against Elizabeth's right cheek.

"Please..." Frank spluttered, shaking his head in disproval, fixing his damp eyes on his wife.

Without a moment's hesitation, Darren shoved the blade deep into the old flesh and pulled it downward, causing Elizabeth to erupt in agony. Cries of such had become fulfilling during Darren's recent activities.

As Elizabeth's tiny frame kicked about on the

chair, Darren lifted the blade and proceeded to carve another slice onto her face alongside the other. He then joined them at the top and bottom and quickly removed the piece of skin from Elizabeth's distraught face.

"Stop this, we have money," Frank yelled. However, he knew deep down his offer wouldn't help in any way.

Darren tossed the piece of flesh onto the middle of the table and made his way over to Frank while Elizabeth writhed about in pain. The air crashing against the exposed tissue injected throbbing suffering through her.

"You'll pay for this," Frank said. Even though he knew there was absolutely nothing he could do, and he was no match for Darren, however, he still found the words falling from his mouth.

Darren didn't give any reply, he grabbed a wad of Frank's hair in his fist and pulled his head backward.

Darren carried out the same procedure on Frank and once he removed the piece of skin, he shoved Frank's head forward from his grasp.

The elderly couple sat in shock, looking towards one another, any form of hope had long evaporated as their blood made its way down to the floor.

Darren returned to Elizabeth and placed the piece of her husband's face on the table in front of her. He fetched the needle he had brought with him and began to thread it. Ensuring he doubled up like before as it minimised his stitching becoming undone.

Holding the needle and long thread in his right hand, Darren carefully picked up Frank's skin and pressed it against the open wound on Elizabeth, which instantly caused her to toss about on the chair.

"I thought you loved him, what better way to do so by making him a part of you forever," Darren smiled, as he tried to control her gyrating head.

Vomit threatened Frank's throat realising what Darren was going to do. "Stop this," he cried, the blood flowing steadily from him and patting gently against the floor beneath.

"Hold still or I'll shove this needle through his goddamn eye!" Darren commanded, finally having his fill of toying with Elizabeth.

The warning sent chills through her. Elizabeth didn't want to be the cause of any further torture placed upon her husband, so she did her best to comply with her instruction.

She sat as still as possible, feeling the wet, blood-soaked side of the flesh make contact with her own. The sensation and thoughts of what was happening were urging Elizabeth to cry out in horror, however she held it together for the sake of her husband. Her love for him outweighed anything she was going through.

The piece of skin didn't slot into place perfectly nevertheless it didn't matter as Darren began to force the needle through both pieces and pull them together.

Elizabeth released a few whimpers during the

process, but mostly maintained her composure while keeping her glaze firmly on Frank, who couldn't believe what he was witnessing.

Darren stood back and admired his work. Although the edges did not align, he was happy with his work. He then turned his attention to Frank.

"You better hold as still as she did, or I will kill her right now in front of you," Darren warned, taking hold of Elizabeth's skin and holding it to the exposed wound on Frank's face.

Darren once again began to stitch it in position. Each push of the needle and pull of the thick thread through the hole it created caused Frank to wince, but as with his wife, he made it through it with very little movement.

As the couple took in the sight of one another, each couldn't establish which hurt more, the knife wounds or the pain caused by the stitching.

"Isn't it amazing how, if not rejected of course, the skin will heal, and you'll have someone else as a part of you?" Darren said, taking in the sight. "Can either of you feel the piece I've just attached?"

Both Frank and Elizabeth took a moment to digest exactly what Darren meant.

"Well?" Darren asked once again in a raised tone.

"What do you mean?" Elizabeth quizzed, breaking the silence, the tears continuing to flood her face.

"Can you feel this?" Darren spat, quickly reaching across the table, taking hold of the flap of skin he had just attached to her between his index finger and thumb.

The stress placed on the stitches holding it in place sent a vibrating sting about her face.

Darren pulled the new piece of her flesh outward, to be sure it wasn't in contact with the tissue beneath it, as he knew the original piece of Elizabeth underneath would still cause hurt.

Darren pinched the skin as hard as he could and awaited a reaction to appear on Elizabeth's face.

"So… anything?" Daren asked, glaring towards her.

The only pain Elizabeth could feel was from the initial cut and stiches, the area Darren was squeezing was alien to her and she just answered, "No."

Had he been fully open, Darren would have revealed that is was what he expected even before he tied them to the chairs, but he needed to know for sure.

"Interesting, how about you," Darren responded, releasing Elizabeth and doing the same thing to Frank.

He too felt nothing only the injuries Darren inflicted upon him only minutes before, to Frank the piece of his wife's skin fixed to him may as well not even been there at all, which he conveyed clearly to Darren.

Again, this observation confirmed what he had expected.

"You see, maybe if we allowed your new procedures enough time to heal, I suggest you probably would began to feel some kind of sensation through it," Darren stated, wondering if he harvested some of their skin for himself and used it in the same way, would it help him finally feel something, however he knew the answer was *No,* his condition went far deeper than that. "We don't have time for that so we'll have to move on. Maybe a bigger piece might work,"

These words crashed against the couple like a tonne of bricks. Their bodies were frail enough without being put through the physical torment being placed upon them.

All rationale in Darren's mind pointed towards a negative result following the next experiment he had in his mind, however, his obsession continued to drive him forward.

Darren turned and flicked on one of the rings on the electric cooker beside him. He slid the frying pan onto it as the surface slowly began to glow beneath it.

Darren spun back to Frank and pushed his chair closer to the table.

"What are you doing?" Frank asked, his face burning, the blood falling from it had slowed somewhat due to the flesh being pulled together.

"Put your left hand on the table," Darren instructed, picking up the axe.

"What?"

"DO IT!"

Darren had tied the couple just above their elbows, so they were still capable of moving their hands freely, to a point.

Frank slowly raised his shaking limb and placed the palm of his hand flat on the table in front of him.

Darren suddenly grabbed Frank's arm, pulled it further towards him and with one violent swing, Darren introduced the edge of the axe to the elbow joint which emitted a loud crunch.

Frank spat in anguish and rattled uncontrollably on the seat, while Elizabeth looked on in horror.

Darren raised the axe and swung it downward once again, repeating the loud thud against the table. He fetched the knife and ran the blade across the sleeve of the shirt Frank was wearing. He then rolled up the remaining piece of material towards the bicep to reveal the severed arm.

Without a moment's hesitation Darren grabbed the handle of the pan, which was by then piping hot and forced it against Frank's brutalised arm.

The smell of burning flesh and the sound of the limb sizzling against the hot steel filled the room alongside Frank's screaming.

"Please stop, you're going to kill him," Elizabeth begged.

"This will stop the bleeding," Darren replied, a crooked smile displayed across his face, relishing the hurt he was causing and the soundtrack accompanying it.

Darren returned the frying pan to the cooker and made his way over to Elizabeth.

"Your turn."

Elizabeth gulped down the dry lump in her throat,

thinking of the added torture she was about to experience.

"Stop. We can talk about this," the elderly woman pleaded, waiting for her husband to raise his head after the extreme shock to his body.

Darren didn't pay any attention to the begging, he forced her arm up onto the table, as he did with Frank, and chopped off her left limb at the elbow. The pain was like nothing Elizabeth had ever experienced and the only thing she could do was cry out for help as loud as she could. The volume of her bellowing hit its limits once again when Darren cauterised the wound.

Hearing the remainder of the bone in Elizabeth's arm scrape against the base of the pan, Darren wondered what it must feel like. Seconds later Elizabeth passed out due to the overwhelming experience.

Darren turned to Frank whose head was still slouched, he was still breathing, evident by the expanding and collapsing of his chest.

Darren picked up Elizabeth's torn arm and placed it beside her husband's, the liquid contents from both still trickling onto the white tablecloth.

He turned his attention to the drawers below the sink and pulled them open. Darren retrieved a pair of scissors and carefully removed the sleeves from the chunks of meat he proudly displayed in front of him.

Darren tossed the waste pieces of clothing to the floor and studied the cuts he had created.

Not bad at all, Darren thought to himself running his hands along the edges which seemed to be workable.

With Elizabeth currently passed out and Frank semiconscious, it gave Darren the perfect opportunity to examine the severed stumps remaining on their bodies.

To his delight Darren found that they too were in a condition he could work with.

Without wasting another moment, Darren grabbed Elizabeth's forearm and held it up against Frank. Although it was slightly thinner, he knew he could pull the skin together and stitch it in place.

Darren carried out the same test with Elizabeth and was also confident he could secure her husband's arm upon her with very little trouble. He laid both limbs back onto the table and began to thread the needle once again.

If he managed to suitably attach the limbs and wait a few hours, he wondered if it would yield any results. The fractures in Darren's mind by then fully consuming his rational thoughts. He grabbed a huge wad of kitchen roll from beside the microwave and patted it against both limbs to seep up the excess blood which was still weeping from them.

Glancing towards the wedding rings on each hand Darren grinned to himself, knowing the pair would have never imagined they would end up like this and now they were going to wear each other's wedding bands in a sadistic way.

I suppose each one of them now truly knows the other loves them, Darren thought, after witnessing the display and pleas they had portrayed for one another.

Not wasting any more time, Darren shoved the needle through the flesh on Elizabeth's dismembered arm and held it in position against Frank, who was still unaware of what the vicious man was about to do to him.

Darren pushed the point of the needle through Frank's charred flesh which instantly shot him back to life.

Frustrated by his flaying about, Darren introduced a closed fist to his temple, instantly rendering Frank unconscious.

Darren, continued to secure the limb in place by pulling the needle and thread around the entire arm, until he finally had it crudely fixed in position. Pleased with his work, he quickly turned his attention to Elizabeth.

Darren fetched Frank's chopped limb and held it against Elizabeth's stump. Pausing a moment, Darren was sure the couple had held each other's hands over the years, however now they would have their soulmate's body part attached to them forever.

While Darren worked his way through attaching a piece of Frank to her, Elizabeth groaned, he prepared to beat her unconscious again, however she did not open her eyes.

After pulling the skin together and threading it in place, Darren sat down at the head of the table and took in the sight in front of him.

He concentrated on the limb swapping he had carried out and visualised them becoming animated as the pair became aware of their surroundings once more.

Without warning, Darren beat his hand hard against the table, causing it to rattle on the solid floor beneath it, hoping it would shock the couple to life so they would begin to move their newly attached limb about, however, nothing.

Darren reached out, grabbed the arm he fixed to Frank and raised it a little. Everything seemed to be still in place, it was still fully connected so he lowered it carefully and carried out the same examination on Elizabeth.

Darren considered shaking each of them about until they were coherent, but after some short contemplation, he opted to allow the pair time for their newly acquired body pieces to heal somewhat and take hold naturally.

He stood, checked the restraints on both individuals, checked the area for any means of escape, locked the back door to the property and made his way into the sitting room.

Darren quickly noted the numerous family photographs proudly displayed on all four walls and the many ornaments sitting upon the mantelpiece above the still burning fire.

Although time was not on his side, Darren decided to leave it until daylight broke to see if the old couple would come to and if they would be able to feel their new limbs.

Lowering his mutilated body onto the sofa, Darren fetched the remote and moved his way through the channels, finding nothing to maintain his interest.

Flicking off the television, Darren sat, an arm resting on each arm rest, waiting for the first sign of daylight to march its way across the night sky.

He looked down towards his hands, hands which had caused so much agony and torment over the last number of weeks, however there was no stopping now. People knew who he was and what he had done, the only goal Darren had was to keep murdering his way through the community before the Gardaí caught up with him. If they did, it would take a lot of effort to bring Darren down and his reign of horror to an end.

He turned his attention back to the pictures on the walls encasing him. All were a combination of smiles, hugs, important occasions, and other memories of times long past.

Maybe they can be next, Darren thought, stopping at a picture of Frank and Elizabeth in a group photo with who he could only assume to be other family members. *Wouldn't be smiling after I smashed their teeth in and ripped their jaws off their faces,* ran through Darren's mind, visualising their reactions and the harmonies of screams that act would create around him. He quickly dragged his attention back to the current situation he was in, Darren knew he couldn't let his wandering thoughts get the better of him while he was in the middle of his current procedure.

Pulling himself up from the seat, Darren checked on the old couple and quickly found them both still unconscious, both limbs still in the same position he left them. He glanced to the clock on the wall to find it was just about to strike midnight, and turned back to Frank and Elizabeth slumped over in front of him.

Studying their time-worn faces, Darren speculated what was going through their minds. He questioned how they would react once they realised what he had done to them.

A chilling breeze and rain beat against the side of the house as daylight tried its best to pierce through the thick, dull sky the following morning.

Darren was raiding the fridge when he heard a low, muttered groan being emitted behind him. He turned to witness Frank beginning to find his bearings.

"Morning," Darren said, gulping a slice of cooked ham down his throat.

Frank did not respond as he rapidly squeezed his eyes together to help him wake up quicker.

Seconds later, Frank tried to lift himself from the chair. Realising he couldn't, Frank then tried moving his arms which instantly shot an injection of pain through him as the stitches stretched under the weight of the inanimate lump of meat crudely attached to him.

Looking down, Frank took in the horrific

operation he had been subjected to. His eyes snapped across the table towards his wife who seemed to have undergone the same procedure and it was at that moment he spotted a piece of him connected to his wife.

"What the hell have you done?" Frank cried, still praying he was still in the middle of a terrible, cruel nightmare.

"Try to move it!" Darren instructed, dismissing Frank's shock.

The old man stared at the obscene body mutilation carried out on him while the pain, unlike anything he had ever experienced before pulsated from it.

"Is she dead?" Frank wondered, noting Elizabeth hadn't moved since he came to.

"Not yet, but I will strangle the life from her if you don't try to move that arm!"

The threat to his beloved wife gave Frank the energy to begin to move the amputated portion of his arm.

"Not that piece. Move the fingers!" Darren commanded, his eyes fixed on the old woman's digits attached to Frank.

"What?" Frank asked, turning his head back to Elizabeth, hoping he would be greeted with her looking back at him. She wasn't, and a part of him didn't want her to wake up to undergo further suffering.

"I'll chop every limb off her if you don't move the damn fingers," Darren roared, slapping Frank firmly across the face.

Although it was an impossible request and with his beloved wife in mind, Frank turned back to Darren and concentrated on something he knew was unachievable.

Meanwhile, Darren stared at the lifeless digits in front of him.

Seconds passed and still nothing as Frank's mind raced, knowing his attempts were going to be greeted with anger.

Without warning Darren stabbed a blade down into the back of the dead limb connected to Frank. "Useless," he said, removing the knife from the withered flesh, the blood oozing from it as he stood from the table.

"What are you doing?" Frank asked, watching Darren step over and stand behind Elizabeth.

There was no response from Darren as Frank took in the sickening sight of the blood-soaked blade hovering close to his wife.

"What you're asking me to do is impossible," Frank spat, the pain from his wounds continuing to echo through his body.

Darren responded by gripping a handful of Elizabeth's soft, grey hair and pulled her head upright.

"Please don't," Frank begged, the tears pouring down his face at the thought of any further harm coming to Elizabeth.

Without further hesitation, Darren forced the tip of the blade into the loose flesh around the old woman's neck, quickly out the other side, causing the crimson body fluid to gush from it.

Frank cursed him for what he had just done and tried his best to fight his way out of the firm restraints, but it was no good.

"What are you going to do about it?" Darren laughed. "What can you do?" His tone becoming firm again as he moved over towards Frank.

Knowing he was helpless, Frank fixed his gazed upon Elizabeth and visualised her beautiful smile, an expression which always made him feel better no matter how bad his day was.

"I love you," Frank said, moments before Darren plunged the knife into the frail man's chest.

Frank kicked about, gasping for life, while Darren removed the blade, stabbed it deep into the old man's chest again and once more, just for good measure.

Listening to the knife puncture through the chest cavity brought some satisfaction to Darren as he took his place at the table again and placed the implement down in front of him.

Although the elderly man was unable to move the digits on the limb which had been attached to him, Darren wondered if the operation had been allowed more time to heal, would it have been successful? His logic would say no, however his obsession allowed no room for conclusion.

Darren looked to Elizabeth and then to Frank, the silence of the corpses ringing through him. He looked towards the blood gathering on the floor beneath the table and grinned, knowing that the liquid played a vital role in maintaining life.

The recent results and intrigue made Darren contemplate his next move. If he subdued individuals and carried out the limb swapping exercise, then allowed enough time for the wounds to heal would they take to their new hosts?

Knowing the risk of moving about in daylight was a lot more significant, Darren decided to wait in the dead couple's house until evening and darkness arrived.

Ensuring he gathered up the items he brought to the house with him, Darren placed them safely into his pockets and sat with the corpses until night fell.

At various stages during his stay, Darren reached across to each limb he had attached to the opposite body, inspected it and moved it about on the table, hoping in a way it would react. However, neither of them did.

Checking beyond the window later that evening, Darren was satisfied it was dark enough to conceal his movements away from the house.

He made sure to leave the lights on before he closed the back door firmly behind him to give the illusion all was normal within.

Stepping out into the darkness Darren knew it wouldn't be long until, Jennifer and her son's bodies were found, and the bodies of the couple he just massacred. He needed to decide who was next and where to carry out the act, because once the bodies were uncovered, the Gardaí would no doubt investigate his property first.

Chapter 16

The Gardaí were called to Jennifer's home soon afterward, due to concerns raised by people in the area that the mother of one had not been seen in some time.

It was a bright, cool day when the first two Gardaí on the scene received no response at the door. After they inspected the house for any suitable entry point, the only option was to break in through the door and it was then they witnessed the grotesque sight within.

The area was immediately sealed off for a technical examination, however, the Gardaí were confident who the perpetrator was.

Sergeant Moore, a small man who was facing retirement soon, ordered two Garda cars to go immediately to Darren's home and carry out a full search of the area. The final orders he gave to the five Gardaí who stepped up to the task was to bring Darren in, or down, at all costs.

They wasted no time departing towards the home of the man who had weaved a nightmarish cloud over the community.

By then people began to congregate outside Jennifer's house as word of the recent, grisly discoveries spread through the town and surrounding areas like wildfire. These individuals were instructed to go home so the investigation could be carried out unhindered and for their own safety.

What the Gardaí, and locals, didn't know was that Frank and Elizabeth, two beloved members of the community, further victims of Darren's cruel acts, were decaying, unnoticed in their home.

The Gardaí quickly reached Darren's property, cut the huge lock off the gate and slowly made their way up the long driveway, with minimum lighting used to help cloak their arrival, so he couldn't make good his escape if he was there.

Unknown to them, Darren had predicted their movements. He gathered all the implements from his house, placed them into a bag, hid them in the wooded area adjoining his land and was currently observing the two cars creep up towards his house from afar.

Who do they think they are, no one has any idea what I am trying to achieve! Darren thought to himself, as he watched the squad cars pass by him, unaware he was hiding in the thick undergrowth.

The vehicles came to a halt in front of the structures which had been witness to so many atrocities.

In a synchronised action, the drivers of both cars activated the high beam headlights while the other Gardaí leapt from them, followed by the drivers. Two made their way to the front of the building and three ventured towards the rear, after quickly inspecting the shed beside the boarded up house.

Although in a group, each Garda felt their nerves battling against them, knowing what Darren was capable of and what he had done to their colleague in the shed just a short distance away.

Both entrances were inspected and were found to be still firmly barricaded. It was following this when it was noticed that one of the boarded up windows had been tampered with.

"Over here!" One of the Gardaí called, his torch light fixed steadily on the broken barrier.

He was joined seconds later by his colleagues, who all stared at the void, each wondering what further horrors lurked inside.

"Darren, come out with your hands up where we can see them," the nearest Garda called out, while the unit waited for any indication of movement from inside.

There was no response.

Still unaware they were the ones being monitored from the cover of darkness a short distance away. "Darren, we have the place surrounded. Don't make things any harder than they need to be. Come out right now," the Garda instructed in a firmer tone. Not one of the five pairs of eyes moved from the smashed piece of timber and glass in front of them.

The group waited for any sounds to echo from within the dark hole in front of them, however there was no evidence of any scuffling or escape attempt heard.

"We'll have to move in," one Garda uttered, his

attention still fixed on the house.

These were words not one person in the unit wanted to hear, however they all knew the statement was correct.

"Okay everyone needs to be on their toes!" Another Garda said as he slowly made his way over to the window.

He gripped the thick, broken timber board and tried pulling it from the window frame. It bowed, however it didn't release its grip.

He was joined by another Garda, who took a firm hold of it with him and pulled, while the closest Garda kept her torch on the task at hand and intermittingly scanned the surrounding area.

With a loud crunch, the barricade finally released its hold and it was tossed to one side as the pair took a few paces back from the house.

"Darren, if you are in there this is your last chance to come out. There is nowhere to go," the closest Garda said.

Again, there was no acknowledgement from within the building, so it was decided to proceed with entering and secure the property.

Stepping over to the windowsill, the closest Garda shone the torch about the room he was about to climb into to make sure it was safe to do so.

Satisfied Darren wasn't hiding in the corners of the first room, the Garda carefully climbed passed the shattered glass and stood waiting for his colleagues to join him inside. Although they all wanted to apprehend the monster who terrorised the area and killed someone close to them, the Gardaí needed to execute the search safely.

Seeing the female Garda, the last to climb into his property, Darren fetched the small axe he had stolen and crept his way over to the window.

Meanwhile, the Gardaí inside his house slowly made their way from room to room, clearing each one as they did, while they prepared for Darren to leap out at them at any time from the shadows to injure them or try to make his escape.

"Clear!" The female Garda called in the last room, after she checked behind the door leading into it.

They found evidence Darren had been on the property, however it appeared he was long gone. The only area they had left to check was the attic.

Each person beneath the entrance in the ceiling leading up to the space above their heads held their breath, each wondering who was going to volunteer to pop their head up there. Because, if Darren was lurking in the attic, surely when he heard the board leading to his hiding place being removed, he would lash out and attack as ferociously as possible. However, the entire house needed to be checked before they could widen their search.

"Okay, lift me up," one of the Gardaí said, standing underneath the attic door.

Two of the other male Gardaí standing closest to him stepped forward and carefully hoisted him up onto their shoulders.

Batons at the ready, the other Gardaí concentrated their torches on the timber covering the entrance to the attic.

Reaching up slowly, the Garda placed his palms against the board and turned to his colleagues to ensure they were ready for whatever was about to happen. With the nod, he pushed upward, quickly removed the piece of timber and threw it to the ground.

The Gardaí supporting him placed their hands beneath his feet so he could stand up, allowing him to peep over the ceiling into the attic.

"Darren, if you're up there, there is nowhere to go. Come on out, let's not make this any worse!"

Hearing no reply, he knew he had to make sure the space was empty.

Holding his breath, torch shaking slightly, he placed his empty hand onto the wooden frame and began to raise himself towards the opening. All this while visualising Darren slicing his exposed fingers off his hand, as he did so.

No one spoke as his eyes passed the ceiling level and up into the attic, the sweat bulging on his brow.

Shining his torch around the area, there was no sign Darren was there and he started breathing a little easier as he was lowered back to the floor below.

Finding nothing in the attic, the Gardaí began to make their way back outside to search the adjoining land.

The female Garda was the first one to reach the

window they used to gain access. She handed her torch to one of her colleagues and began to climb back outside when suddenly there was a loud, violent thud as the Gardaí watched her body slump and become limp before them.

Unware to them, when her head had come into view, Darren swung the axe downward as hard as he possibly could, introducing the edge of it against the back of her neck.

"Fiona!" One of the men called, witnessing the axe connect with her neck once more, causing her head to dangle further from her drooping body.

Her partner took hold of her blood-soaked shoulders, quickly followed by the other men and pulled her back inside the deranged man's home, as her head flopped about.

The group looked on in horror as they lay their colleague on the floor, her life fluid still spouting around their feet.

One of the Garda's attention quickly shot to the window he just pulled Fiona from to see a figure shoot past it.

"Sick bastard," he yelled, and ran towards the opening leading outside.

He was quickly restrained by the other men, one of them saying, "We can't just climb out there blind Tom. He'll pick us off one by one."

"We should have made sure it was okay!" Tom replied, breathing heavy, pulse racing. He was a burly individual and the most senior of the unit who didn't want to just stand by with a dead woman at his feet, the perpetrator just a few feet away.

"I know, but he tricked us. We need to be careful."

"There is more of us. We need to get out there!" Tom replied, shrugging away the grip of his colleague. "I'm not just going to stand here!"

Although they didn't voice their opinions, each one of the men felt the exact same way as they watched Tom walk over to the window.

"I'll go first," Tom said, determined to get his hands on Darren, adrenaline and anger pulsating through him.

He swiftly checked outside the window and shone the torch about the area as much as possible. Although he and the other Gardaí wanted to bring Darren to justice for the cruel acts he committed, Tom didn't want to end up with his head semi-detached from his body like the lifeless woman on the floor behind him.

Satisfied Darren wasn't in the immediate area, Tom climbed from the house to the open darkness, quickly followed by the rest of the Gardaí.

Each slight movement from the heavy night around them caused each man's attention to snap towards it. They knew Darren wasn't far away and needed to apprehend him before they, or anyone else fell victim to him.

"Stay sharp. He is out here somewhere," Tom said, feeling the sinister pair of eyes fixed firmly upon him.

Without warning, they witnessed Darren sprint

from behind the shed into the dense woodland around them, triggering the same reaction from the four Gardaí.

After following the sounds of Darren making his getaway, a heavy silence cascaded down around the men who paused and shone their torches quickly about the area, trying to pick up Darren's trail.

All looked alien to them, and each swipe of the torch light seemed to highlight a different aspect of what was around them.

Darren had a great advantage in this environment. Over the last several weeks, he built up a basic understanding of the layout and the beams of light emitted from the four torches pinpointed exactly where each man was. He also had collected the bag of items he had hidden earlier, so he had everything he needed.

"Where the hell is he?" One of the men whispered, slowly taking a step forward, listening for any movement.

Fetching a rock, Darren ducked down behind a fallen tree to the left of the group pursuing him.

Tightly gripping the bloodied axe, he tossed the stone deep into the thicket of trees behind him, instantly causing the flashlights to swing in its direction.

Darren watched as the lights slowly made their way towards the approximate area where the stone landed.

"Careful, we don't know what he has out here,"

one of the men said, eyes surveying as much as possible.

They continued to the location they assumed the noise came from, each Garda ready to leap into action if they witnessed Darren making his getaway once again from the shadows.

Peeping over the large tree trunk, Darren saw that each light was spaced about twenty feet apart, the closest one just a short distance away from him by then, so he quickly concealed himself once again before he was spotted.

Waiting patiently, Darren listened as the footsteps got closer to him.

Suddenly Darren sat up and swung the axe violently against the Garda's left ankle, instantly causing him to fall over towards him. In a flash, Darren introduced the edge to the back of the man's head, cracking it, before sprinting off again into the darkness.

The initial cries from the man, caused all torches to snap towards him, as his colleagues witnessed Darren splitting his head open.

The dwindling unit raced over to the rapidly twitching body, which stopped moving seconds later, indicating Darren had taken another life.

Tom didn't stop, he followed Darren who was gradually disappearing in front of him into the woodland.

"Tom, wait!" Called one of the other men, as the pair raced off, some distance behind him.

By then Tom had come to a halt, Darren had escaped once more and had retaken the role of stalking the Gardaí.

"Can you see anything?" One of the Garda's said to the other, trying to locate any sign of Tom ahead of them.

"No, not one thing! We need to catch this lunatic!"

The Gardaí scanned the area around them and were greeted with heavy undergrowth and a labyrinth of trees shooting their branches in all directions.

"I think Tom went this way," a Garda said.

Rounding one of the thick trees he was greeted with a shear drop as he plummeted and came to a sudden stop with a loud thud on the hard ground below.

"Brian!" The other Garda yelled, seeing him instantly fall and disappear from sight.

Aiming the beam of light downward he could see Brian slowly twisting in agony with one shin bone bursting through his pants and his other leg bent into an unnatural position.

"Stay still. I'm coming down," he yelled, trying to find a safe way down to help his colleague.

Meanwhile, Tom continued through the natural maze, squeezing his baton, hoping he would lay his eyes on Darren again.

"All alone I see," a voice called from obscurity.

"Come on out. Try doing the same to me!" Tom roared, determined to break the baton off Darren's skull.

"What exactly do you think you can do to me?" The voice continued, getting closer to the defiant Garda.

"Show yourself and you'll find out!"

Seconds later, Darren stepped into view a short distance away, ensuring to hide the bag of implements. He pulled down the hood covering his head to reveal a crooked, stitched smile displayed across a disfigured face.

Disbelief splashed across Tom taking in the sight in front of him as the stitches holding the chunks of flesh Darren had pulled into position stretched under the pressure of his facial movements. However, he wasn't prepared to let the appearance of the monster in front of him stop him from punishing Darren for what he had done.

"Do you even realise how messed up you are?" Tom said, gripping the baton tighter, his shock turning back to anger.

"Maybe I'm the normal one!" Darren spat back.

Without hesitation Tom raced towards Darren and swung the baton as hard as he possibly could, striking the bark on a large oak tree due to Darren quickly side stepping the effort.

"Even slower than I thought," Darren smirked, pulling the small axe from the front pocket on his hoodie. "Look, it still has her blood on it," holding the steel up to his face, eyes rigid on Tom.

Tom shot to Darren once more, swinging with all his rage, but Darren caught his wrist in the process, blocking the attack. Instantly Tom cracked the torch in his left hand against Darren's temple, causing his head to jolt, a trickle of blood to flow and the sadistic smile to grow larger.

"Come on, surely you can hit harder than that?"

The Garda swung and connected with Darren's skull again, the thud of the blow echoing through the area.

Astonished, Tom looked into eyes which became more intense in front of him.

In an instant Darren quickly drew back and smacked his forehead hard against the bridge of Tom's nose, flattening it across his face.

Tom stumbled backward, vision blurred, as Darren advanced towards him.

"Try harder!" Darren said, grabbing a handful of hair, cracking Tom's temple with the handle of the axe, dropping him to the ground causing him to drop the torch in the process.

"You won't get away with this," the words stumbled from the Garda's mouth.

"I already have."

Darren swung at Tom, however he managed to roll out of the way just in time. Gathering himself as best as possible, he pulled himself back up to unsteady feet, baton still in hand.

Tom lunged at the hellish man and the pair wrestled about in the light cast from the torch laying on the ground beside them.

The bulky Garda managed to overpower Darren

and they both fell to the soil beneath them. Tom, luckily landing on top, began beating the fiend as hard as his hand would allow with the baton.

Darren couldn't contain his laughter as the blunt implement connected with his head, neck and arms as he tried to deflect the blows.

Although he did not feel the impacts, Darren wasn't stupid, he knew he couldn't continue to take the beating for long before his body failed.

By then a bloodied mess, the tirade of aggression still raining down upon him, Darren jostled about with all his strength, eventually forcing his thumb into Tom's cheek, where his upper and lower jaw met and pressed and pulled as hard as he could.

Tom winced in pain, giving Darren the opportunity to throw him off and reverse the position.

Darren wasted no time punching Tom's head as hard as he could, luckily for him, Darren had dropped the axe when he was originally flung to the ground.

Suddenly Darren was tackled off Tom.

Turning, Darren saw, by then the last uninjured Garda trying to help his colleague back to his feet. By that stage there was so much blood spouting from both men, it was difficult to identify who had the most injuries.

"Someone else wants to join in the fun eh?" Darren said, undeterred by the additional wound inflicted upon him.

He began stepping towards the two Gardaí,

knowing the fight would still be almost even, due to the beating he just gave Tom and judging by his composure, the Garda was barely conscious.

"Stay away from him Stephen," Tom mumbled, saliva and blood falling past his lips, his jaw clearly dislocated.

Stephen suddenly eyed the axe laying on the ground a short distance away in the bright torchlight. He eased Tom against a tree, his face unrecognisable. Stephen grabbed the weapon and turned back to Darren.

Certain some of his injuries were serious, Darren was confident time would heal them and darted towards Stephen.

The pair tussled with one another briefly before Stephen pushed him away, creating some distance between them. He swung the axe, Darren leaning back just enough to watch the blade swing past him, then lunged at Stephen again.

Darren grabbed Stephen and tried to force him to the ground, however the Garda beat the back of the axe down between Darren's shoulder blades knocking him down to his hands and knees. Stephen then swung the axe with as much force as he could and drove it deep into Darren's torso, lodging it in place.

Seeing the injury didn't drop him to the soil fully, Stephen punched the back of Darren's head violently and collected Tom's baton close by.

He looked on in disbelief as Darren stood back upright.

Casting his eyes downward, Darren saw the axe had been buried in him and he was losing an extreme amount of blood. He knew if he stayed any longer, he would die.

"Pointless," Darren yelled before turning and sprinting into the dark woodland behind him, snatching the bag of supplies.

Stephen contemplated giving chase, however he couldn't leave his injured colleagues behind him. He would never be able to live with himself if they also died due to him leaving them to try catch Darren.

"Did you see that? He didn't feel it," Stephen said, helping Tom back up to his wobbling legs.

"That's why he is so dangerous. He doesn't feel anything," Tom replied, wiping the thick, flowing blood from his mouth. "Come on, we can't let him get away. Where is Brian?" He asked pressing on after Darren, wondering why Stephen was on his own.

Stephen quickly grabbed Tom's arm, feeling the determination in him Stephen said, "He fell. He is in a bad way back there."

"Fell?" Tom asked, turning back to Stephen.

"Yeah, his legs are broken. We can't go after Darren. We need back up to deal with this. Let's call it in. Even though he can't feel it, Darren won't get far before he collapses and hopefully dies out here."

Although he didn't like the thought of giving Darren the opportunity to create some distance between them, Tom decided to take the advice of his colleague.

The Gardaí radioed for assistance as they both ventured back through the darkness to the location where Brian was laying, his body broken.

Meanwhile, Darren raced through the heavy undergrowth, his insides quickly spilling from him as he beat away the natural barriers jolting out from the trees around him. Happy he had run long enough, Darren stopped at the next opening he found in the naked canopy overhead. He unzipped and reached into his pocket and from it pulled the needle and thread.

Using the intermittent moonlight above, Darren pulled the needle from the spool, which thankfully he had already threaded.

He grabbed the handle of the axe, ripped it from his body and took off the hoodie.

Looking down, Darren took in the outline of the decaying faces of his victims he had meticulously sewn to his torso. He then caught sight of the wound spilling his blood to the ground below.

Without wasting any further time Darren clutched a handful of skin, the injury in the centre of the clump of it and began to stitch as best he could in order to prevent his death.

Watching the needle flash in the moonlight, Darren wondered what damage had been inflicted within him. He could do his best to seal the outside of his body, however any vital parts broken inside were out of reach, and it wasn't like he could just stroll into Accident and Emergency for treatment.

After making several crude stitches across the large laceration, Darren turned his attention back to continuing his escape from the location.

He threw the filthy hoodie back over him, collected the items at his feet and disappeared into the darkness.

Chapter 17

Snapping sounds echoing upstairs through the dark hallway awoke a woman from her peaceful slumber.

Louise Fitzgerald was a twenty-five-year-old local business woman, who lived a short distance from Arklow.

Shooting up on the mattress beneath her, Louise listened for any further noise from the floor below her, as she become more rigid each passing second.

Moments passed, which seemed like hours as she waited for any sign of a break in.

Hearing nothing further, Louise reached across to the bedside locker beside her to collect her phone. However, as her palm was greeted by only the cold timber, she remembered she had left it downstairs after falling asleep on the sofa.

By then Louise was unsure if it was just a dream she had been experiencing which had awoken her.

A further five minutes or so passed by with no further cause for alarm and she kicked herself for being so silly. Needing to use the bathroom, Louise reached towards the locker beside her bed once again, this time flicking the switch on the small lamp.

Enjoying a subtle stretch and long yawn, she climbed to her feet and made her way to the toilet at the opposite side of the hallway.

Walking past the stairs, Louise couldn't help but glance down into the blackness, her mind tormenting her with the image of a person standing at the end of steps glaring back up at her, thankfully it remained just a thought as she closed the bathroom door behind her.

Soon afterwards Louise switched off the bathroom light, happy that she was about to enjoy another few hours sleep before she had to get up. Stepping back towards the top of the stairs, Louise heard the message tone sound from her mobile phone. Due to it being such a late hour, she decided not to go down and collect it. However, another strange noise ricocheted through the house again, paralysed her to the floor.

Louise, although every part of her told her not to, cast her eyes down the stairs, which by then seemed a mile long.

Her heart thumped loudly, while she gripped the top of the banister so hard it turned her knuckles white. Listening attentively, Louise studied the darkness below her for any sign of movement.

Suddenly Louise heard heavy footsteps quickly make their way across the wooden floor in the sitting room. Her eyes and mouth painfully widened witnessing a figure sprint up the stairs towards her.

Louise spun to her right and raced towards her bedroom, closing the door and locking it behind her just in time to see the figure lunge and hearing it crash hard against it.

The terrified woman stood away from the barrier between her and whoever had broken into her home as a deafening silence descended.

Louise looked on in horror witnessing the handle slowly move downwards. She considered hiding, however whoever it was, knew she was in there.

"What do you want? Get out now, I'm calling the guards!" Louise roared, with as much venom in her words as she could muster.

"They will never get here in time. Plus, I doubt you have two mobile phones!" A voice growled, only millimetres from behind the door.

Desperation ran through Louise realising whoever it was must have heard or seen her phone notification downstairs.

"What do you want?" Louise roared once again, her mind racing for any form of escape.

There was no response.

Without warning there was a loud wallop against the door which caused Louise to leap. This was quickly followed by another and another, as whoever was outside tried to kick their way in.

Louise glanced towards the window opposite her, but she knew she couldn't jump, as the ground below was covered with concrete and it angled away from the house, creating a longer drop. She was convinced she would break at least one leg or worse, leaving her helpless.

Instead, she switched off the bedside light and hid behind the door as the beating continued upon it. Her plan was to run out and downstairs once the person began to search the room for her.

The thuds became heavier and harder until Louise began to hear the lock give way. She wanted to scream but held her nerve.

Seconds later the door violently swung open, almost cracking her in the face.

Silence.

Covering her mouth, Louise fixed her eyes upon the edge of the door, waiting for the dark figure to dart into the room to begin their search.

However, seconds passed, then minutes, while she remained in position, wondering why the intruder had not entered the room.

She listened attentively for any movement but there was nothing. Complete silence.

Louise adjusted her position as quietly as possible so she could look through the crack in the door beside her. Still nothing, no movement whatsoever.

She could feel her body rattle in fear, but Louise could not let it overwhelm her.

More painstaking moments crawled by and Louise rationalised whoever it was may have realised they had gone too far and decided to make a run for it.

Louise slowly stepped forward, fighting against her instinct to stay in position and peeped around the door to be greeted with total darkness.

She knew she needed to get downstairs to her phone to call the Gardaí for help.

Taking a deep breath, Louise stepped out from

behind the door, taking note of the many foot marks indented upon it.

She reached for the light switch and she heard something run toward her from the hallway outside.

Without having any time to react effectively, Louise turned to witness two hands reach for her neck from the darkness.

She was forced to the ground with a loud thud, and following some brief struggling, her wrists were quickly lashed together. The intruder spun Louise around onto her back and stared down at the fear-stricken woman.

"Please..." Louise uttered, staring up at the cloaked figure standing over her.

Louise was hoisted up and over the person's shoulders and carried downstairs towards the kitchen.

Her captor flicked on the kitchen light and sat her down in front of the table.

Louise felt the vomit in the back of her throat eyeing the hideous, twisted face looking back to her. She realised it was Darren.

Although she had heard about Darren and the terrible acts he carried out on his property, she hadn't time to process that it was possibly him who broke into her home.

"I have money," Louise said, countless possibilities running through her mind, all concluding with her death.

There was no response as Darren began to empty the contents of his hoodie and bag onto the table in front of him.

"You don't have to do this. Leave and I won't even call the guards, I promise, I'll forget this ever happened," Louise pleaded, hoping her words would influence the monster.

"Stop begging. You are wasting your time trying to change something you can't," came the response.

Turning her attention to the items on the table, one of the many things Louise noticed was the box of sleeping tables, Darren had stolen from the pharmacy, positioned closest to her.

"What are you going to do?" Louise asked, turning back to Darren, watching the stitches on his face stretch as an oozy substance trickled from the areas where the needle had punctured the skin.

"The only thing left to do!" Darren replied, pausing a moment, "You are going to become very, very special. You will help me live on through you."

Before Louise had any time to rationalise what he was saying, Darren quickly opened the box of sleeping tablets, clicked a few into his hand and stepped over to the bound woman.

"Open your mouth!" Darren instructed.

Without giving her anytime to react, Darren grabbed a handful of Louise's hair and pulled her head back towards him with so much force it caused her to cry in pain.

Darren stuffed the tablets into her mouth and proceeded to hold it shut while covering her nose.

Louise fought against Darren with all her strength

in order to get out of his evil grasp, but it was no use. He was too strong.

Staring into Louise's wide, panic-filled eyes, Darren waited until she could no longer fight the urge to swallow. Once he was sure she had ingested the tablets, Darren grabbed her mouth and pulled it open to double check.

Louise tried to stand, however she was quickly and firmly forced back down into position.

Darren waited, never taking his eyes off Louise, until he knew the tablets he forced into her system were starting to take hold of her.

Louise battled as hard as she could against the building drowsiness, however as further time past and the tablets were digested, the tiredness rapidly overcame her.

Darren shoved the table to one side and lay Louise flat on the floor.

He then began to undress her and threw her clothing to one side. Once Louise was in her underwear, Darren pulled his clothes from his body to reveal huge swelling around the axe wound inflicted upon him. Darren was confident he was slowly dying, however it had no impact on him.

Darren searched the kitchen and found bin bags under the sink. He placed them over the kitchen table as a makeshift tablecloth. He retrieved the knife he brought with him and flicked the switched on the kettle beside the sink. He needed the blade to be as clean and sterile as possible before he got to work.

Once he was satisfied, Darren dried the blade, knelt beside Louise and began to cut into her body.

Chapter 18

An immense grogginess was quickly counteracted by excruciating pain as Louise awoke from her deep, involuntary slumber. She tried to move, however she was secured in position and the attempt caused the pain to greatly intensify.

"You're awake and more importantly, alive," Darren said, sitting on the chair opposite her.

"What have you done, how long have I been here?" Louise asked, her head fixed firmly towards the ceiling.

"Let's get you some nutrition, it will help your body heal," Darren replied, making his way to the fridge.

"Heal, what do you mean heal?" Louise asked, her mind racing. The agony growing.

Darren did not answer. He rummaged through the contents of the fridge and pulled out some packaged ham and cheese. He sliced the meat and cheese into small pieces and squatted down beside Louise's head.

Darren held a slice of ham to Louise's mouth and she couldn't help but notice the small trickle of blood slowly running down Darren's wrist towards his palm. She kept her mouth closed.

"Eat!" Darren instructed.

Knowing she was in a helpless position, Louise

parted her lips and took the food into her mouth. After she swallowed the piece of meat, Darren wet her lips with water, then pushed the cheese into her mouth.

After she ate, Darren stood and placed the food onto the table. He picked up a blister pack of sleeping tablets once again, clicked more into his palm and stepped back over to the captured woman secured to the kitchen floor.

Louise had no energy to fight, and felt she was already close to death, so sleep would be a welcome release as she willingly took the tablets.

It was quite some time before Louise regained consciousness.

Again, the pain was unbearable, and she couldn't move any part of her body.

Turning her eyes to the right, Louise quickly noticed Darren laying on the kitchen table, now closer to her. She could see he wasn't wearing his hoodie and his arm and other areas of his body which she could see were missing huge areas of flesh.

Her worry skyrocketed further witnessing the plastic tube which was attached to Darren's arm, filled with a crimson liquid, making it way down toward her.

Suddenly Darren moved on the table.

"What have you done?" Louise whizzed.

"I'll live on and feel through you. Even your children will have some of my DNA in them,"

Darren said, after a brief silence, "You are truly my greatest accomplishment and your pain will also be mine."

A chill through Louise as she conjured countless images and ideas in her mind of what he had done to her.

Louise attempted to quiz Darren further, however she was unable to get any more information from him.

Watching his hand become limp and his breathing cease some time afterward, Louise knew Darren was dead. However, she was still trapped and in immense pain. She thought of crying for help, however she knew the chances of anyone hearing her were very low and she didn't have much energy.

Louise decided her only way of possible survival was to conserve her strength and hope someone would miss her and come searching soon.

Several days passed before the alarm was raised that Louise had not been seen in a while and the Gardaí were called.

They quickly made their way to Louise's home and the Gardaí were greeted by a house with all the curtains pulled across its windows and a securely locked front door.

Due to the nature of recent events and a crazed murderer still on the loose, the Gardaí wasted no time and kicked in the door.

They slowly made their way inside, searching and

clearing the house room by room until they were greeted with the horrifying, vomit inducing scene in the kitchen.

They found Darren dead on the kitchen table and Louise on the floor in her underwear, hands and ankles tied and over her body were a number of leather belts, which were placed over the woman's body and nailed to the tilled floor.

The Gardaí raced to Louise to find the presence of a very weak pulse.

After calling for back up, they began to remove Louise's restraints, however, they couldn't help but keep viewing the grotesque surgery carried out on her.

Darren had removed huge pieces of his and Louise's skin from various parts of their bodies and stitched his flesh onto the gaping wounds on Louise. He also had a syringe placed in his arm, attached to a medical tube, which was connected to Louise. Darren had placed a tiny nick in Louise's wrist and as a droplet of body fluid passed from her, it was to be replaced by his.

When the paramedics arrived, they treated Louise for extreme malnutrition, shock and pain.

She was removed from her home and brought to the nearest hospital for further examination.

Surgeons were horrified at the skin swapping procedure that had been performed on her. Due to her current, weakened condition, surgery was deemed out of the question. The doctor's main concern was keeping her alive and they fought hard to battle against any advancing infection.

Following a few weeks in hospital the wounds would heal and she would hopefully regain her strength, however Darren was now a part of her. It had been pure luck that their blood types were a match and Darren had achieved his final wish.

His blood was inside and flowing through her, his skin wrapped around parts of her and each time she looked in the mirror Louise would see a piece of Darren staring back at her. This final deed proved that the only true way Darren's flesh would experience any type of feeling, was that it had to be taken away from his body and supported by another.

Louise would need a lot of therapy to help her manage what he had done to her in some way and if she indeed went on to have a family, she would in his cruel way, be passing Darren's DNA onto her children.

Doctors would need to help Louise manage her life after surviving such an unspeakable body mutilation rather than her taking it, when she found out the true extent of what he had done to her. They knew her mind would be overwhelmed as they slowly revealed that Darren had replaced a large percentage of her skin with his own, the shock of which may drive her over the edge.

However, no matter what her ultimate decision with her life would be, she had possibly suffered the cruellest act of Darren Kelly, and the community would never be the same. Darren's horrendous, sadistic legacy would live on for many years to come.

The End.

About the Author

Chris lives in County Wicklow, Ireland. He has been a horror fan for as long as he can remember. Within Their Screams is his sixth release and doesn't plan to stop anytime soon.

www.chrisrushauthor.com

Other Books by Chris Rush

FOLKLORE
ALL SHALL SUFFER
THE LEGEND OF LOFTUS HALL
13 DEAD
FOLKLORE: THE SECOND TALE

Printed in Poland
by Amazon Fulfillment
Poland Sp. z o.o., Wrocław